THE COTSWOLDS WEREWOLF

and other stories of Sherlock Holmes

Peter K. Andersson

Edited by Alice Smales

Paperback ISBN 9781780925417
ePub ISBN 9781780925424
PDF ISBN 9781780925431

Published in the UK by MX Publishing
335 Princess Park Manor, Royal Drive,
London, N11 3GX

www.mxpublishing.com
Cover design by www.staunch.com

Contents

The Adventure of the Cotswolds Werewolf

I.	A Quiet Corner of England	4
II.	The Reverend's Diversion	21
III.	The Boom of the Bittern	36
IV.	A Grotesque Interlude	59
V.	The Wild Man	71
VI.	The Secrets of an Old Shepherd	86
VII.	A Tale of Slaughter	95
VIII.	Wolf's Bane	110

The Adventure of the Velvet Lampshade   117

The Adventure of the Missing Mudlark   150

The Adventure of the Forking Paths   180

The Adventure of the One-Armed Pugilist   204

The Adventure of the Cotswolds Werewolf

I. A Quiet Corner of England

In the early autumn of 189—, my friend Sherlock Holmes and I decided to spend a restful week at a hotel in the heart of the Cotswolds. It was a Friday when we set out from Paddington station with our luggage neatly stowed in the overhead shelves of a first-class compartment, and the lazy September sun enveloping the brownstone buildings of inner London in its shuddering rays. I was looking forward to our trip with some trepidation, having recently witnessed how my good friend had descended into some form of indefinable ennui. As usual, it was the result of lacking mental stimulation, although this time the customary episode of boredom and apathy had given way to a lengthy bout of depression and anguish. The only possible cure that occurred to me was a retreat into the countryside. At the back of my head, however, I feared that this was an all too conventional solution to an unconventional problem.

During the entire trip, Holmes remained silent. He avoided my gaze as he had for days, and devoted his time to uneasy meditation and to the study of a black clothbound volume that he had acquired a few weeks earlier, but which he refused to allow me a closer look at. He had consented to the trip quite reluctantly, of course, and as I was unsure myself of the efficacy of this remedy I wavered slightly, but then I thought there would be no point in me appearing hesitant, and so I stood firm, until Holmes capitulated one day, sighing from the depth of his armchair: "Well, I might as well do nothing there as here." Those were the only words I had heard him utter for several days when we embarked on our journey.

As we left London behind us, and the industrialised landscape of the Thames valley slowly receded, the greenness of the surrounding countryside increased, reminding me how long it had been since I last allowed myself a good breath of country air. The sight of the green and pleasant hills seemed to make Holmes slightly more animated as well, and eventually he closed his book and settled himself to enjoy the view, letting the little volume slide into the side pocket of his Norfolk jacket. I was, of course, delighted, but refrained from commenting on it so as not to make him self-aware.

In the late hours of the afternoon, we arrived at Moreton-in-Marsh, in the heart of the Cotswolds. The tiny station consisted of a small wooden hut on either side of the railway tracks. The platforms were peopled by a diminutive assembly of station masters, porters, odd-job men and a couple of shunting horses waiting to become useful. Having disembarked, we were promptly accosted by a young cab driver whose keen eye had evidently managed to spot the two most lucrative clients in the vicinity. We had no reason not to take him up on his offer of a ride, and followed him to his horse and trap on the far side of the platform. Our goal for the journey was a little hamlet called Upper Slaughter, the seclusion of which had been guaranteed to me by a colleague of mine, who had recommended the little village inn that went by the name of The Briar. Our cabbie deposited us in front of its thatched exterior, and I noticed in the corner of my eye how Holmes descended from the vehicle, looking about himself with an air of something that could either be skepticism or foreboding.

The inn was located in the absolute centre of the village, along the stretch of a gravelly village street lined by little quaint houses. A few yards away there was an intersection, and the connecting road rose up on a hillside, the top of which was adorned by a small but sturdy medieval church.

"Well, what do you think?" I asked Holmes.

"I think…" He sighed and frowned. "I think it's going to rain."

I looked up at the sky and realised that his conclusion was no act of genius. The outlook was positively dismal. We lifted our luggage which had been thrown down on the ground by the amiable cabbie, and hurried inside. It took a few seconds for my eyes to get used to the darkness that enveloped us. We had come into a small antechamber whose walls were covered in a wainscoting of dark oak, and the only source of light was a paraffin lamp standing on a squat side table in one corner. The experience was something very similar to entering a tomb. Through the open door behind us we could hear thunder, and soon the rain started pouring down. The darkness of the room was amplified by the closing of the door by a little figure that moved through the shadows, but soon stepped out in front of us holding a flickering candle.

"Good afternoon, gentlemen," it said. "I fear our weather is not the most welcoming."

The voice was an old lady's, and as she turned up the flame of the paraffin lamp, we could gradually make out her features, a look of kindness framed by a couple of round cheeks. The combination of intimidating darkness and the gentleness of the welcome confused me as to how I should respond.

"You are our guests from London, I take it?" she said.

Holmes gave me a sidelong glance, wordlessly commanding me to be our spokesperson.

"We are," I said, failing to imitate the woman's enthusiasm. "I am Dr John Watson. This is Mr Holmes."

"Ah, yes, the two gentlemen. Welcome to the Briar. I am the owner and proprietor of this establishment, Mrs. Faversham."

And with these introductory remarks, the usual series of courtesies had commenced. Holmes played, as was his custom, a very minor role in this interchange. He could be cordial and sociable at times, but mostly, and more frequently of late, he abhorred the superficiality of idle chatter. He had explained his stance on it to me a number of times, and I could understand it to a certain degree, but my feeling was always that this attitude constituted something of an arrogant perspective on daily life and the simple people. "We cannot go through life talking profound philosophy and displaying a full conscience in every single moment," I would say. "We need to get on with our lives! And what is more, the simple people, which, to be honest, is the overwhelming majority of humankind, enjoy life without philosophy or analysis." But the discussion is an eternal one.

Hence I could seldom experience moments like this without feeling just a little irritated at Holmes' arrogance and impatience, but I said nothing, reminding myself that this was the beginning of a slow process towards recovery. Mrs. Faversham showed us to our rooms, after pointing out the location of a comfortable parlour and dining room either side of the dark reception that we had entered into. The moment Mrs. Faversham reached out the key to Holmes, he snatched it from her, voicing a quick "Thank you, Mrs. Faversham!" and hurried into his room, slamming the door shut behind him. I said something about a foul temper as explanation to the slightly shocked landlady, and then retreated into my own room.

I suppose I had taken for granted that I would meet Holmes at dinner that evening, but when he subsequently failed to make an appearance, it all seemed quite obvious to me. Would I see anything at all of him for the next few days? Would he eat? Would he leave his room? Would he leave and not come back? The reasons for worry piled up, and I recognised the burden of stress upon my own shoulders. I tried to tell myself that what I could do at this time was to concentrate on my own relaxation. And so I tried to forget Holmes. He is a grown man, I thought, and can take responsibility for himself. I did not know if it was true.

Coming down to dinner, I found my way into the dining room through a suite of darkened parlours, cluttered with odd furniture, sheepskin rugs and stuffed animals that looked as if they hadn't seen a duster for years. The only sound came from an old grandfather clock, ticking as noisily as if it was some large piece of industrial machinery, and the rain on the windows. The dinner service had already begun. Mrs. Faversham was sitting at the head of the table, flanked by a motley collection of old men and women. They were introduced to me as Colonel Draycot, a retired serviceman, Mr Bevis Tipsy, an amateur draughtsman, and Florence Gilchrist, a local widow. I was no longer a young man, but I felt positively puerile in the present company. The dinner commenced without further ado, and I was introduced to the guests, gradually acquiring an insight into the serene but tedious goings-on of the locality. I received the impression that this quiet corner of the world was a place where relatively undistinguished but well-off people came to spend their autumn years, indulging in the usual activities of fishing, painting indifferent watercolours and aimlessly documenting the local plant life. Colonel Draycot turned out to be nurturing an interest in folklore, and spent his days walking around the vicinity, knocking on the doors of distant farmhouses and interrogating poor country folk about their local traditions, folksongs and whether or not they believed in fairies. Mr Tipsy likewise spent his days trotting about the wet grasslands with an easel under his arm, and was currently engaged in a project wherein he was making drawings of straws of grass, the description of which I nodded in response to with feigned fascination. And Mrs. Gilchrist talked to us about knitting, which seemed to be all she was interested in talking about.

As we moved into the parlour for a drink, we were joined by the local vicar, who was my age, and seemed a decent sort of man. His name was Tibbins, and he was a jovial and amusing fellow. Making a welcome change from the others, he was kind enough to take an interest in me, and it wasn't until he had been able to work out that I was the Watson who, with an increasing infrequency, was chronicling the achievements of my investigating companion that the rest of the company was struck with a sudden keen curiosity. I was unwilling to say too much on the matter, however, and even managed to stifle Mrs. Faversham when she was about to announce that I was here in company with Holmes. When they realised they were not going to get anything interesting out of me, they soon tired, and the topic of conversation changed.

Only when the guests had left, leaving me alone with Mr Tibbins, did the conversation turn to juicier topics. Having reclined into a couple of armchairs with a decanter of port between us, we mused on the weather, the current state of the empire and the recent deplorable efforts in British cricket. Quite soon, I couldn't help but notice, however, that something was on the young vicar's mind.

"Is something troubling you, Mr Tibbins?" I asked.

He slid a hand across his furrowed brow, and shot me a weary glance.

"Well, since you ask," he said, "and since you seem to be a man of the world, you might oblige me with a fresh perspective on a business that has been on my mind of late."

"I am intrigued. Tell me about it."

Mr Tibbins emptied his glass of port and chose his words.

"There is, in the adjoining valley, an old established sheep farmer called Parker. He is one of the most successful sheep farmers in this part of the country, and his sheep graze all over the surrounding pastures. Last week, it came to my attention that four of his sheep had been found killed in the next valley. And not only that, their deaths had been executed in the most gruesome manner, leaving beyond all doubt that they had been ripped apart by some savage animal. I did not visit the spot myself, but my wife, who is knowledgeable in anatomy, saw the remains, and locals tell of a gruesome scene, body parts and pools of blood spread across a considerable area."

"My God. How atrocious."

"That is not all. Since then, I have heard stories from other villages in the vicinity, of other sheep farmers having their sheep butchered in this way. And there is even talk of a cow in Staunton that came back from grazing with bleeding wounds made by an animal's claws."

"But what sort of animal is there in these parts that would inflict such injuries?"

"That is exactly the part of it that is vexing me."

"England has no large predators. Foxes, surely, but what sort of fox would attack a large cow? Unless... unless of course it is some exotic animal that has escaped from a zoo or a circus, or even from the menagerie at some local estate. Holmes and I once had reason to visit an estate that had both a baboon and a cheetah roaming free in the grounds!"

"Indeed? Well, that sounds like a reasonable explanation."

He rubbed his chin.

"But you don't seem inclined towards it," I remarked.

"Well. There are no zoos or menageries in this area as far as I know. And circuses seldom visit this part of the country. We're too far away from the towns. Then again, I wonder... I wonder..."

"Come now, Mr Tibbins. There is a theory of your own taking shape in your head. But you seem unwilling to share it."

"It is only a fancy. You would laugh at it."

"Not at all!"

"Well, being a doctor and a gentleman from the city, you must understand that our country ways might seem foreign to you, ancient even."

"My good vicar, I am enlightened enough not to discard provincial people as savages just for being simpleminded."

"Of course. I should not have underestimated you."

"So...?"

"So. Being a man of God, I have seen some strange things in my times. And even though I might still pass for a young man, I am not unfamiliar with the old ways and the ancient roots of my belief. And that is probably why I must attribute some of this to the principal antagonist of my organisation."

"You mean...?"

"Satan."

"Ah."

"I hope I do not shock you, Doctor, but when something like this happens, raw and brutal violence in its purest form. It must be the work of the evil one."

"I am not judging you, vicar, but it is an old maxim of Holmes', that we should start by eliminating the most

12

reasonable explanations, moving methodically towards the less likely ones, and not consider them until the others have been falsified."

"I appreciate that, Dr Watson, but I must confess my position is ambiguous. For a man of the cloth, how unreasonable or fantastic is the belief in the intervention of the devil into the world of humans? What am I supposed to believe? I am also a man of reason, and I believe in science and empiricism."

"Well, I could not advise you in theological matters, but I know that there is no point in worrying before one has all the facts. I take it a formal inquiry is being conducted, so maybe you should curb your misapprehensions until you know what comes out of it?"

"You're probably right, Doctor. Whenever I relapse into talk of devils and demons, I hear the echo of my father's voice. It's frightening, isn't it, how we all turn into exact copies of our parents as the years go by?"

I smiled, and, for the first time in a few minutes, so did he. He declared his intention to call it a night, and I thanked him for his company. He thanked me for reassuring him about the sheep massacre, and then he was on his way. It had stopped raining, but outside it was pitch dark and I wondered how he would ever be able to find his way home. I climbed the stairs while slowly unbuttoning my waistcoat, feeling tired but also quite at peace with myself and the placid surroundings I had found myself in. On the way to my bedroom, I passed the door to Holmes' room, and paused. I leaned in towards the door but could hear nothing. I even went down on one knee to peer in through the keyhole, and I could just make out a faint light within, but there was neither sound nor movement. I decided to allow Holmes to do his own bidding and went to get some sleep, which I was sure Holmes would not.

The next morning was grey and cold, but I awoke with a zeal that invoked me to go for a long walk directly after breakfast. At breakfast, I asked Mrs. Faversham if she had seen Holmes around, and she replied that he had requested that his breakfast be sent up to his room. When I asked her how he had requested this, she said that his door had been opened slightly when one of the chambermaids had been on the landing outside, and a gentle voice had asked for breakfast to be sent up, a message which the maid had promptly passed on to Mrs. Faversham. Content with the recognition that this was Holmes' wish, I did not make any further inquiries, and thus set out, packing a small sandwich that I had assembled from what the breakfast table offered, a pair of binoculars and a map of the area which I had obtained from Stanford's in London as sole preparation for the trip.

I began by exploring the village, climbing the little hill to the church, meandering through the alleyways looking at the quaint cottages, and gradually moving further and further away from the centre of the village, through copses and across streams, passing an Elizabethan manor house in the distance. Eventually, I came to the top of a ridge, which offered a picturesque view of the village I had left behind me and, when I turned, of the next valley, where moors and grazing pastures stretched out in green waves. I recalled the vicar's story of the previous evening, and wondered where the tragedy had taken place, but all I could see were peaceful flocks of sheep scattered around the valley. I trotted down the slope and scared a few sheep off as I advanced, beating the grass with a dry stick that I had found in a grove of trees half an hour before.

I walked for at least an hour, maybe two, my feet feeling nothing but wet grass and the occasional sheep dropping underneath them, until I had negotiated the length of the little valley that had lain before me, and was looking back across it from the top of a low hill which bordered on woodlands. Here, a narrow footpath followed the edge of the forest, descending into a basin where I fancied I could see some houses. Closer inspection revealed a little village made up of a cluster of cottages, one of which, to my considerable satisfaction, was an inn. I considered the sandwich in my pocket, whose appearance had not improved from being flattened and dampened in the course of my exertions, and decided that such an industrious day as this required sufficient nourishment.

The inn was housed in a little thatched cottage with a roof that looked like it had caved in on a few places. The sign outside read "The Green Man," which struck a suitable note of primitivism. I had to stoop to be able to get below the straw that covered the low door. Inside, a row of men was standing by the counter, all dressed in muddy boots and hardy tweed clothes ripped and frayed here and there from walking through thorns and undergrowth. Two of them appeared to be farmers, and the third one I recognised as Colonel Draycot from the night before. The topic of conversation was familiar to me.

"It's a bear, I tell ya!" said one of the farmers, pounding his fist on the counter. "A great vicious bear. They spotted one up in Yorkshire only a few weeks ago."

"Come now, Marcus," said the other one, a short and chubby man with a kindly face, "there are no bears in England. That's old wives' tales."

"The only thing I know is that what happened to those sheep could not have been done by anything smaller than a bear."

The farmers became quiet and brooding, leaning in over their pots of beer and seemingly looking for answers to their questions in the black surface of the beverage. I ordered a cottage pie from the landlord, and Colonel Draycot invited me to take a seat with him by the fireplace. I sat on a large wooden chair that creaked pleasingly, and the colonel reclined into an armchair before starting to fill his pipe.

"Tell me, doctor," he said, "what do you think of this place so far?"

I confessed that I had been here so short a time that I had not yet been able to form an opinion. But the colonel persisted.

"But if you were forced to say something, describing it in just one or two words, what would you say?"

I shrugged.

"Well, my first impression was that it was a bit gloomy. Gothic, even."

"Yees." He seemed to analyse my words, syllable by syllable. "That is what most people say. Indeed, that is what people have been saying for centuries. Did you know that when Pepys came here, that is exactly what he wrote? 'A village for walking corpses', I think was the way he put it."

He chuckled.

"And why do you think this is?" I asked, realising this was something he was most keen on discussing with me.

"Having looked a little into the history of this region, I suspect it has something to do with Upper Slaughter's old reputation for being home to witches and warlocks in the sixteenth and seventeenth centuries."

"Really? Any truth to this reputation?"

"Oh yes. This is where Matthew Robbins, the famous witch finder general, held some of his most gruesome witch trials. He managed to make three women confess to the most heinous deeds, including abducting young children, boiling and eating them."

"Good Lord!"

"But the village had already had a long history of dodging the watchful eye of the religious establishment. Some believe that they never really converted to Christianity, secretly worshipping the old pagan gods in the privacy of their homes. Even if this reluctance to conform to the Christian practices was expressed only in the most modest ways, you can imagine the reaction of the witch hunters when they stumbled upon a place like this."

"I should think they would be quite pleased with such a discovery."

"Exactly! Even though whatever they found could barely make a case for indecency. But it was a basis for spinning wondrous tales that gripped the imagination of the time. A woman in the village who used herbs as medicine could be easily accused of witchcraft. A local tale about a mythical creature living in the forest could be turned into suspicions of a shapeshifter among the inhabitants."

"Shapeshifter?"

"Oh, it is a common term within the occult. It denotes a person who is able, by magic, to change into an animal or some fantastic monster. There are many tales from the Middle Ages and the Reformation about such people. The most common form is the werewolf myth."

"Of course. But when I think of werewolves, I associate it with a continental tradition. Surely our beliefs are limited to hobgoblins and Robin Goodfellow?"

"Not in the least, Doctor. British folklore is hardly lacking in monsters and demons. Have you not heard about the Hedley Kow or the dreaded basilisk of Shropshire? And it is also an often overlooked fact that many of those who were accused of witchcraft during the time of the great witch craze were men, and that those men were often accused of being werewolves."

"That is most interesting. Do these beliefs still exist among the common folk, you think?"

Draycot glanced at the two farmers at the counter, whose conversation had turned to more worldly topics —on how best to fertilise hops, from what I could hear. Draycot leaned towards me slightly, and lowered his voice.

"To be honest, Dr Watson, not really. But it is fascinating to observe how an event like the recent sheep killings may stir up the old superstitions."

He gave a faint smile, and I nodded. Then my lunch arrived and the colonel excused himself. He seemed an agreeable old man, after all, although of a sort with which I have become all too familiar, those who can only appear agreeable when talking about the things that interest them.

Having satisfied my appetite, I resumed my walking and wandered around the area for the remainder of the day. I saw a lot of sheep, and one or two cows, but no wolves and no bears. As dusk was falling, I returned to the village and to our little inn, which was a most welcome reunion after my escapades. After freshening up and changing my clothes, I decided to look in on Holmes, whose wellbeing had been greatly on my mind during the day's meditations. The landing was quiet as I approached his door, and his room remained silent even after I had knocked. I knocked again, and then I thought I heard a rustle inside, as if from something dropping or falling over. I grasped the door handle, and realised the door was unlocked. Upon opening it, I was met with darkness. The curtains were drawn and only a flickering candle by the bedside interrupted the gloominess. I noticed that Holmes' luggage was mostly unopened, and that his travelling clothes had been thrown over a chair in a corner of the room. Holmes himself was lying in the bed, the thick covers drawn up to his neck, and the pale little head that was sticking over the top had such an empty apathetic look that it seemed to me the severed head of a corpse. But somehow I knew full well that he was neither dead nor unconscious.

I proceeded to the windows and opened the curtains slightly.

"How has your day been?" I queried, acidly.

Holmes shifted to one side, moving his face away from me.

"Well, I've had a fantastic day," I said and pulled up a chair. "A long vigorous walk across the heath, a good ale at a local inn and some chats with the locals."

"Sounds ghastly," Holmes murmured.

"To someone who thinks almost everything is ghastly, it does, I suppose. But there are things here that would interest you too. A murder mystery, for instance."

Holmes pulled his covers up over his head.

"Does that not tickle your curiosity?"

A long silence was followed by a faint reply from underneath the sheets.

"I'm sure it's something very common. A peasant husband beating his wife to death in a fit of jealous rage. A country vicar suffocated in his sleep for the sake of his strongbox."

"Not quite. But I'm afraid it falls a little out of your territory, since the victims are sheep."

"Sheep?"

"The local farmers have had several of their sheep brutally killed by some vicious animal. Virtually ripped apart by the likes of it. My theory is insurance fraud."

"Yes. No doubt that's it. These farmers will do anything to sustain their livelihood."

"Now then," I said and rose. "Will you not dine with me this evening, Holmes?"

"Certainly not."

"Come, come. This charade is quite tedious. I know that your depression is fading away, I recognise the signs. Had you been at the bottom of the pit you would hardly have spoken to me."

Holmes was silent.

"I shall go downstairs and will expect you at dinner in ten minutes," I said sharply.

The silence continued, although, as I walked out of the door, I imagined I could hear giggling from underneath the covers.

II. The Reverend's Diversion

The following morning, I felt as though Holmes' ennui had been transmitted to me. When I saw the sunlight trying to creep in through the gaps at the edges of the curtain, I buried myself deeper in my pillow and tried to fall back to sleep. The physical strain of the day before had taken its toll on my leg muscles and I could feel them pulsating, as if gasping for breath. I remained in bed well into the course of the day, and it was approaching eleven o'clock when I descended the stairs to see if breakfast was still available. I met the parlour maid in the foyer and asked her if it would be possible to have something cold to eat, and she scurried off to accommodate my request. Stepping into the sitting room, I noticed a pile of newly arrived morning papers on the sideboard, and positioned myself in an armchair to look through them. Most of them were a few days old, and some I had even read already before leaving London, but the later editions brought me up to date on the recent affairs concerning the prime minister's strive to secure home rule for Ireland as well as further details regarding the Featherstone tragedy.

After a few minutes, the parlour maid brought me some sandwiches with mustard and cold beef, and I muttered some words about the house seeming rather empty this morning. "Yes sir," she said. "Mrs. Faversham has gone into town. The other gentleman and yourself are currently the only guests, so the work is slight at the moment."

"Yes. And 'the other gentleman' is not much of a burden as long as he stays in his room."

"Oh, but he went out early this morning."

"Who did?"

"The other gentleman."

"You mean the man who arrived with me? Mr Holmes?"

"Yes! There's no one else, is there?"

"But I mean… Did he say anything?"

"Not a word. Me and the other girl were scrubbing the front steps when he just hurried past us with not so much as a good morning! He was carrying a shoulder bag and was wearing quite heavy walking shoes, and he hurried off towards the fields."

"Did he indeed? And when was this?"

"Around seven o'clock, I should think."

I leaned back in my chair, looking no doubt rather puzzled. The girl curtseyed and went away. The news made me wonder, first whether the girl could not be mistaken, and then whether Holmes' departure was a bad omen, meaning that he had left for London or gone out hoping to disappear in the wilderness. I consumed my breakfast as quickly as I could and then I went out onto the village street, not in order to trace Holmes, but to get some sort of overlook of the situation. There, I was reminded that it was Sunday. The church bells were ringing and people from all over were creeping out of their little cottages to attend service. These people had been virtually invisible up until now, as if congregating in the street was something done in all other country villages, except this one. The stream of people was so all-encompassing that I, being in a state of bewilderment and apathy, allowed myself to be carried off with it, and slowly stepped towards the little stone path that climbed up the hill in between the little houses, leading to the church.

The service gave me the opportunity to see the vicar at work. His sermon was brief but astute, the topic being the virtues of contemplation; and the unassuming, pensive nature of his character that I had born witness to on our last meeting shone through favourably in this context. At one point, however, about halfway through, he was interrupted. He was doing a short digression upon the lives of the medieval anchoresses, when suddenly a couple of young men in one of the back benches started to bleat like sheep. The sound began as a faint noise accompanied by giggles from their friends, and as their initial shyness was supplanted by daring inspired by the encouragement of the other young men, the baa-ing grew louder and louder. Until, that is, it was brought to a full stop by someone at the other end of the church who let out a piercing wolf's howl that echoed over the heads of the churchgoers. After this, the congregation was completely silent, apart from a few lingering giggles.

The vicar's reaction to this insubordination was to cast a solemn glance at the assembly, looking not unlike a strict headmaster. For a moment I thought he would comment on the prank, but he did not, and I concluded that this was probably the wisest thing to do, a reprimand being likely to encourage rather than deter the pranksters. Sitting quite far back, I had a good view of the young men who had made the sheep noise, but I could not determine who had made the responding wolf howl. During the remainder of the sermon, the villagers appeared restless and concerned, as if the lark had reminded them of the dark cloud hanging over the district. As the service concluded and the people streamed out of the church, I lingered, taking a moment to admire the interior of the building. The architecture, as far as I could tell, was Norman in style, and since it appeared so well-preserved, it was strange that the building was not more famous. The frescoes in the ceiling I presumed to be of a slightly later date, although the naïveté of their execution clearly dated them to the Middle Ages. The hereditary grimness of the village that Draycot had talked about was apparent even here. A detailed depiction of the Day of Judgment took up most of the space, and my eyes were drawn especially to a large congress of ugly little devils doing unspeakable things to poor naked sinners and pushing them towards the mouth of hell with pitchforks. There was a scaly little thing sticking long rusty nails into the arms and legs of an innocent-looking young woman, and a slouching little creature covered in fur biting a man's calf with its meticulously painted fangs.

So consumed did I become by this vulgar display that I was quite startled when I heard a voice of greeting and saw that the vicar had crept up behind me. He was beaming and the reason for his contentment seemed to be my interest in the frescoes.

"Aren't they wonderful? It's quite rare for them to be so well preserved, you know. I see it's the little devils that have caught your attention. They are the feature that most people take an interest in. So symptomatic of the human race, wouldn't you say? Perpetually drawn to that which we know to be evil or unhealthy."

"You appear to be in good spirits today, Mr Tibbins," I remarked.

He looked at me, the broad smile broadening.

"Of course. I always feel this way on Sundays. Quite natural for a clergyman, don't you think? It would be strange otherwise."

"Weren't you disturbed by the childish prank carried out by those young blackguards during your sermon?"

He looked to one side, his smile changing into one of impatience.

"No. Well... A bit, perhaps. There will always be contrarians. But I think it is a sign of a deeper concern within the community, one that we will have to deal with. Tell me, Doctor, would you like to come to lunch at the vicarage?"

I didn't want to offend the man by telling him that I had had a late breakfast, so accepted. After removing his ceremonial robes in the vestry, he escorted me out of the church and across the churchyard to the neighbouring vicarage. Here, a number of other guests had already assembled, including Mr Bevis Tipsy and Colonel Draycot, who this time was accompanied by his wife. Mr Tibbins' wife was also there, as well as a number of local wealthy farmers. They were all waiting in the parlour and though Tibbins kindly introduced me to them as he entered, their attention was almost wholly directed at the vicar, whose amiability was unswerving.

Lunch passed without noteworthy incidence. It wasn't until the party was dispersed and people started to withdraw into the sitting room that conversation became interesting. I happened to end up with Mrs. Tibbins, a young attractive woman whose energy and geniality equalled her husband's. It turned out that she took an interest in anatomy and physiology, and though she had never been able to study professionally, she had devoted so much of her leisure to reading up on these subjects that she was as well-informed as any physician. I could imagine boredom setting in on any woman who was a country vicar's wife, shut inside an isolated vicarage all day, and I implied this assumption to her, but she soon put me straight.

"Oh no, I love this village! In fact, I was born and raised not a mile from here, and have known nothing but the Cotswolds all my life. It is lovely country and I do so enjoy walking in it."

"You surprise me, Mrs. Tibbins. You come across as a woman of the world. I should have thought you to be the daughter of an Indian officer or something similar, having travelled and experienced different cultures since early childhood."

"The only experience I have of the outside world is the experience I have acquired from reading books! Maybe there have been moments when I have longed to travel and see with my own eyes the things I have only read about, but at the end of the day, my way of experiencing the world through books is what I have come to be familiar with and love, and so that is good enough for me."

She smiled, giving me immediate proof that what she said was what she felt, and her smile was of such a nature that one could not help but reciprocate it.

"Then if you have lived here all your life and love it so much, what is your opinion on this notion that it is a gloomy and dark place, home to witches and whatnot?"

Now she laughed.

"Oh Dr Watson, if I told you all the things I have heard about this village. Fairytales and ghost stories. But not a single one of all the rumours has any truth to it. Oh, surely, there were witches and witch trials. There was even talk in my own family that my great grandmother was a witch, or at least a wise woman of the old sort, but, you know, in a small and desolate place like this, people need stories like that. If the big world out there refuses to come to this small world, then people have to make up a big world as substitute."

"So you don't incline towards a supernatural explanation for the sheep killings?"

"Certainly not. In fact, I was present when the police came to inspect the cadavers out on the field."

"Really? And why was that?"

"I was asked to accompany them, as my knowledge of anatomy might be of assistance. A veterinarian from a neighbouring village, Dr Spencer, was there also, as well as Parker, the sheep farmer."

"And was the scene as gruesome as I've been led to believe?"

"Oh, by all means. I shall never forget it for as long as I live. Within seconds, I was convinced that this was not the work of any human with a weapon, nor of any animal smaller than a bear or a large wolf."

"But there are neither in this country."

"That is why I communicated to the police my opinion that they should be looking for a passing circus or carnival, for that is the only reasonable explanation I can think of, that the deed is done by a savage predator on the loose."

"Hmm. If only the police out here had the resources to allow an expert, I mean a real expert, a zoologist at least, to have a look at the remains."

"I agree. But I doubt that he would be able to observe anything we have not."

I rubbed my chin. This whole business was very absorbing, and I was sorry not to have Holmes by my side to share my enthusiasm.

"Then you are more of a rationalist than your husband?" I said to Mrs. Tibbins.

"He shares my opinion," she said. "Just because he's the vicar doesn't mean he must look automatically for a supernatural explanation."

"No, I…"

But I refrained from finishing the sentence. It was clear to me that the apprehensions that Tibbins had conveyed to me were unknown to his wife. At precisely that moment, we were interrupted by one of the farmers, an old man with a long white beard, who was sitting at the other end of the room, but had evidently heard what we were talking about. He raised his voice above the din of the room.

"I know who slew the sheep! 'Twas a wild boar. As wild and as beastly as ever you saw. This country used to be overrun by huge and vicious boars. In some parts they remain, old and lonely animals desperate for food. We only need to engage a good hunter to be free of the pest!"

His words gave way to a heated conversation, everyone talking at the same time. Just then, Tibbins put his hand on my shoulder and moved his mouth close to my ear.

"Shall we escape from this chaos for a few moments? I was hoping to show you a little of my art collection. I believe it might interest you, since you seemed so consumed by the church decorations earlier."

I gladly accepted, and he escorted me into an adjoining room, the other guests not taking much note of the exodus. I was happy to take a rest from socialising for a while. The room into which I was shown was a small sitting room, its walls lined with little framed pictures of modest appearance.

"Now, a true art collector," the vicar began, "does not collect art indiscriminately. There must be a theme in the works he acquires. And my theme is something that used to be popular among artists, but which is now, sadly, disappearing from view. My pictures are all fairy pictures."

I approached the wall, and moved slowly alongside it, little picturesque scenes of dancing fairies and elves passing before my eyes. The pictures were all quite small, and only a few of them were oil paintings, the majority being made up of drawings and humble watercolours. It was the collection of a man of modest means, but the achievement lying behind the assembly of these works of art, most of which seemed to me to be of good quality, indicated considerable expertise. It was curious to think, however, that these images of mainly pagan content were the possessions of a member of the clergy.

Tibbins started to guide me around the room.

"This is an early drawing by Hughes, with an exceptional attention to detail. Here we have a preparatory sketch by Paton for his masterpiece on Oberon and Titania. I love the way he has drawn her veil there." He continued to a watercolour where odd-looking little men and women were dancing in the corner of a field. "This is made by an artist who really ought to be more well-known. His name is Charles Doyle and his sketches of fairies are so humorous and light-hearted that they always make me smile. Now next to him we have a little drawing by Richard Dadd, who was quite famous in his time, but who ended his days in an asylum after having murdered his own father. It is strange to think, isn't it, when you look at this lovely scene, that the mind behind it was capable of murder?"

I looked closer and saw a curious picture reminiscent of an Arabian desert camp, but with the Bedouins and camels replaced by youthful men and women, some of whom were holding the reins, not of horses, but of giant-sized snails. They were all apparently waiting for something, but the weirdly drawn eyes of all the characters were slightly angled, making them all look rather sinister. The picture filled me with unease, and I would not have been very surprised to hear that the artist was a murderous madman.

Tibbins moved on, and we stopped in front of one of the few oil paintings.

"Now here we have the pride of the collection!"

It was hardly more notable than the rest, though, due in large part to its small size. Measuring not more than a few square inches, it was a portrait of a man in full figure. At least I thought it was a man, but when I took a second look, I was obliged to change my opinion. He was naked, and his body was covered in a fur that was painted so slightly and in a white-grey colour that made it barely noticeable, looking from afar more like a white glowing light emerging from the figure. But the strangest part of the picture was the face, which was difficult to make out as the brushstrokes were so rough, but whose proportions and red penetrating eyes made him resemble some animal rather than a man. Tibbins looked very proud while I examined this painting.

"Magnificent, don't you think? It is an early oil study by Fuseli, but this particular motive does not, to my knowledge, reappear in any of his other works. I acquired it while on holiday in Scotland. According to the man who sold it to me, it is a representation of a wild man, and legend has it that Fuseli based it on drawings he made of a man who actually existed and who lived in the forests of the Highlands. Be that as it may, depictions of wild men constitute a pictorial tradition recurrent in western Christian art since the Middle Ages, closely related to the portrayal of so-called green men."

I took great pleasure in admiring the reverend while he lectured on his passion, but what he said also awoke my curiosity.

"Where does this interest in pagan traditions come from, Mr Tibbins?" I asked.

He appeared to blush a little, like a naughty schoolboy caught while in the middle of some foolish prank.

"It is a highly scholarly interest, even though I'm an amateur. But I would lie if I were to deny its origins in my childhood."

"Your childhood?"

"When I was a boy, before I found God, I was a stern believer in fairies."

"How charming! And why is that?"

"I saw one once."

He was wearing his usual attentive smile, but for some reason I was quite sure he wasn't joking.

"Really?"

"Oh yes. As a boy, I used to spend the summer at my aunt's cottage in Yorkshire. I roamed free in the grounds of her vast estate, exploring the woods, playing with paper boats in the stream. And one day, a little man appeared amongst the trees. And by little man, I don't mean a midget. He was a vigorous old man of the same proportions as you and me, the only difference being that he was not much bigger than my hand. He smiled at me, and then he darted off in among the trees. I followed him, but he was moving faster and with more agility than any human I have ever met. I could see him a few yards in front of me while running through the forest, but then I couldn't see him anymore, and despite my searching for an hour, he was gone. And that was that. It was a very brief encounter, but I could see him as clearly as I see you know, Doctor."

"That is remarkable."

"It is. But surely your rational mind is looking for the most convenient natural explanation?"

"Well, I really don't know what to make of it. How old were you at the time?"

"Nine."

"Old enough for us not to dismiss it as childish imagination."

"Yes."

"What does your rational wife make of it?"

Tibbins lowered his eyes to the floor.

"To tell you the truth I have never told her. She thinks my reason for collecting fairy pictures is some ambition to get into the mind of the enemy, as it were. Which I suppose it is, on some level. But that's not quite the core of it."

"Why are you telling me this?"

"It's not every day that a man of the world like yourself finds his way to our little corner. There are many distinguished and intelligent people in this village, but to tell them would mean putting a start to gossip. In a little place like this, you have to think twice before revealing secrets."

I was just about to ask him to tell me more, but just then we were reached by noises coming from the other guests in the next room. Tibbins stumbled past me, and opened the door. The sitting room was in uproar; people were standing and talking loudly all at the same time, making it impossible to make out what anyone was saying. As we stepped into the room, I noticed a group of men who hadn't been there before. They looked like working men and they were dressed in dirty outdoor clothing. It was their voices making the most noise.

With great authority, Tibbins calmed the assembly.

"Now now! What is the matter?"

One of the loud men turned to him, his face red with agitation.

"Our sheep problem has just taken a graver turn, sir," he said. "This time it's not sheep that have been murdered. It's a man!"

Some of the people present loudly voiced their concern at hearing this, while others just fell silent. Mrs. Draycot swooned and fell back into her chair, while the present farmers quickly stepped forward and asked to be taken to the scene. Tibbins pleaded for tranquillity, however, and in a few minutes it was decided that only the most agile men were to go out while the others stayed behind with the women, with the exception of Mrs. Tibbins, who was too adamant and persistent to be forced to stay behind. I accompanied the Tibbinses as they rounded up the farmers together with Draycot and the men who had brought us the news. They showed us the way, down the church hill into the village, along the main street, out of the village and into the fields. While walking, Tibbins inquired as to who the murdered man was. A large man who was leading the way spoke up.

"It's one of the shepherds employed by Mr Parker, sir. His name is Dalton."

Tibbins searched his memory.

"Dalton, Dalton. Yes, I think I remember him. Tall and slim, with a slight limp? Goes by the name of Rover?"

"Quite right. You certainly have a good memory, sir."

"I try to be familiar with the people in my flock."

"Rover Dalton was a good and honest fellow. He was an ex-army man, and from what I've heard, he had been stationed over in India."

I pricked up my ears, ever vigilant of fellow campaigners.

"What unit?" I asked.

"Couldn't say, sir. But that was the reason for his limp. An old war wound."

I was just about to remark upon the strange coincidence in that I was similarly scarred by my experiences, but thought it an unnecessary digression in the current situation. We were hurrying across wet grasslands surrounded on all sides by a gathering mist, which enveloped the trees and hid the village from view. As we reached the top of a low hill, the terrain dropped ahead of us, and the man at the front pointed towards the bottom of a small basin, where something was clearly lying on the wet ground. Upon sighting this, we all hurried down the slope, the vicar almost tripping in the excitement. Approaching the bottom, I could see that it wasn't just a dead body lying there. When Colonel Draycot exclaimed: "Who's that with him?" I realised that there was a second figure right beside the outstretched corpse. It was the figure of a squatting man, who seemed to have his arms on the deceased. As we came closer, it seemed to me that he was examining the body at very close range.

"Hey! You there!" shouted our guide. "Get away from 'im!"

The squatting figure stood up and turned towards us, his tweed coat drenched in the rain, with patches of mud at the lower end and his trilby pulled down, almost hiding his face. But I saw who it was. It was Sherlock Holmes.

III. The Boom of the Bittern

The rain was growing more intense, but no one paid any attention to it. Mrs. Tibbins struggled past the congregation of men to get a close look at the body.

"It is not a sight for a lady!" pleaded one of the shepherds, but the woman did not seem to take his opinion into account. She kneeled beside the corpse just as Holmes had done a few seconds before.

"You should pay particular attention to the placement of the head wound," remarked Holmes.

"What are you doing here? Explain yourself!" said Draycot as if he was addressing one of his soldiers.

"He was not here when we found him," said one of the shepherds.

"Sherlock Holmes, at your service." He extended his right arm.

Tibbins took hold of it with fervent enthusiasm.

"Mr Holmes, such an honour! We could hardly have hoped for more ample assistance in this matter!"

Draycot also shook his hand, mumbling something to gloss over his brusque greeting. The shepherds all seemed oblivious to the reasons for Holmes' renown, probably as a result of deficient reading habits. But despite the surprise of seeing Holmes, it was impossible not to register the presence of the savagely mutilated body that lay at our feet. Whatever had been the appearance of Rover Dalton while he was still alive had been obliterated. His head had been bashed in by a violent blow delivered with savage fury. His chest had been ripped open and his extremities were in such a chaotic position, it gave the impression that he had fallen from a great height or been tossed around like a plaything.

"God help us," said Tibbins solemnly.

"We can't let him lie here!" said Colonel Draycot.

"A couple of the lads have gone to the village hall to find a stretcher," one of the shepherds replied. "We'll keep him there until the police arrives to investigate."

Mrs. Tibbins was completely absorbed by the examination of the dead man. She called out to me without raising her eyes.

"Dr Watson! What do you make of it?"

I stepped forward reluctantly, the apparition of this retired soldier lying gruesomely wounded in the middle of a muddy field recalling all too vividly battles I had tried to forget. However, studying the injuries with medical eyes exchanged these thoughts with cold reason.

"It looks to me like the skull has been crushed with a single blow. And, what is more, the blow has been struck from below, which is a little curious."

"Exactly!" said Mrs. Tibbins.

"QED," muttered Holmes.

"The rips on his torso," Mrs. Tibbins continued, "are undoubtedly inflicted by some animal. But what animal could it be? With claws of that size, not to mention the space between them, it suggests a paw the size of a frying pan!"

"I have some experiences of tiger wounds from India," I interjected, "but they are indeed much smaller."

"Perhaps we should ask Mr Holmes what he makes of it," said Tibbins.

All looks were turned Holmes' way. He stood a bit to the side, with his hands on his back.

"I would draw your attention," he began, "not to the obvious aspect of the injuries, but to the surrounding details. Before your arrival, I had an opportunity to inspect the area, and managed to read the signs inherent in the trodden-down patches of grass around the victim. These signs have now been obliterated by all of you, but they pointed towards the presence not of a single murderer and his victim, but of a number of individuals, present here no more than forty-five minutes ago. Several of these individuals were smoking when they were standing here, but the ashes on the ground were scarce, and neither were there any cigarette butts on the ground, which would suggest that most of these people were spectators rather than actors."

"Are you quite sure the footprints are not the traces of the men who found the body?" asked Draycot.

"Yes, I am, as I was present when they found it."

"You weren't!" one of the shepherds protested.

"That I was here does not automatically mean that I was visible. Anyway, apart from these traces, I could find only this."

He held up something old and rusty, reminiscent of a large nail, but I could not see what it was in this gloomy weather.

"What is it?" asked Tibbins.

Holmes looked at it with an amused smile.

"It's a fork."

"A fork?"

Holmes gave it to Tibbins to examine, who then passed it on to Draycot.

"Looks like it's been lying here for years, judging from how rusty and bent it is."

"Yes, one would think so. But the fact is that if it had been lying here for a long time, it would have sunk into the ground, the soil here being so damp. When I found it not two metres from the body, it was lying on top of the grass as if it had been dropped quite recently."

"So what are we to make of it?"

"I honestly have no idea."

"Right." The colonel looked slightly irritated. "Well, is there anything else you would like to call our attention to?"

"No," said Holmes.

"Mrs. Tibbins?"

Mrs. Tibbins had now stepped away from the corpse. She shook her head.

"Good!" Just then, a couple of boys came over the top of the hill behind us carrying a stretcher. "Capital!" the colonel continued. "Well then, I suggest we leave this ghastly place and move the body to a safe location until the police arrive." He became aware that he was holding the rusty fork in his hand, looked about himself in brief confusion, then handed it back to Holmes.

The dead shepherd was lifted onto the stretcher, and the gathering turned into an improvised funeral procession. The Tibbinses stayed behind to explain how delighted they both were to have met Holmes and how much they admired his work. We were both invited to dinner, but it was agreed that we would wait a day or two, considering the tragic state at hand. The reverend and his wife moved along, and I waited until they were at a few yards' distance before I turned to Holmes. He stepped up to me and put his arm around my shoulders.

"Nice to see you, Watson! Where have you been all day?"

"I might ask you the same thing! The last time I saw you, you were positively suicidal."

"Was I really? Is that a medical opinion?"

"Don't plead ignorance, Holmes. You've been morbidly depressed for weeks on end!"

"What can I say, old boy? I'm fastidious in my assessment of the human condition. Far too often, I find it is not up to scratch."

"Perhaps you should lower your expectations," I mumbled.

Holmes let out a loud "Ha!" "Why should I, when I know what amazing and unlikely turns of events it is capable of producing? No no, the world is inventive, but lazy. The episodes of routine and humdrum in between the inventiveness are far too long."

"For a man who takes such interest in trifles and details, you are curiously unappreciative of the little things in life."

"It is because I spend my time looking at the little things that I realise how boring they are most of the time. Believe me, when you know what fascinating inferences can be drawn from a speck of dust, you cannot stop looking at every single speck of dust. But fascinating inferences can only be drawn from one in a thousand specks at best, and so the fruitless search for that one speck invariably leaves me desperate and discouraged. It's horrible, knowing what wonderful things can happen, and then waiting in vain for them to do so."

"I had hoped that this holiday would encourage you to think about other things."

"To me, there are no other things. My philosophy encompasses everything."

"Then there is no escape!"

"You cannot escape from yourself, Watson."

I sighed audibly. Holmes had a way of winning an argument with a very obvious statement, so I ended up looking like a fool. It was very frustrating.

We had reached the fringes of the village, and I could see the men with the stretcher continuing down the village street towards the village hall.

"I think there is nothing more for us to do at the moment, Watson. Let us withdraw to Mrs. Faversham's charming establishment and see if we cannot spend the rest of the afternoon in the company of a fine bottle of port. I will tell you all about my day and I am curious to hear about yours."

Holmes and I settled ourselves snugly in a couple of armchairs in front of the fireplace. The wind and the rain grew stronger, and as darkness fell, the only sign that there was a world outside was the sound of rain blowing against the windowpanes. I started to relate, not only the events of the day, but also more details of what I had experienced since our arrival, and Holmes listened intently. His increasing enthusiasm provoked me, however, and as I came to the end of my narrative, I could not help but ask him about the reasons for his sudden interest in this place and its people.

"Something made your apathy go away last night, causing you to leave your room for the first time since we came here."

"My dear friend," Holmes replied, filling his pipe, "forgive me for toying with you. It is not malice that drives me to tease you like I did a few minutes ago, but you know how I prefer playing mental games to clumsily wording my emotions. In point of fact, I have been far from apathetic in my room, simply absorbed. Absorbed by the study of that fascinating little book I have brought with me, if you remember. It was only this morning that my contemplation brought me out of my room."

"But you could hardly have known that you would go straight out and stumble on a dead shepherd."

"Well, the probability for such an eventuality was not negligible. As a matter of fact, when you told me about the sheep killings last night I wasn't at first very intrigued. But during the night, the scenario stayed at the back of my head, and I amused myself by going through every thinkable explanation in my head. The exercise absorbed me more and more, until sleep proved impossible, and I found myself sitting at the writing desk, making up a list of the options. Your theory about insurance fraud I quite quickly discarded as unlikely, since I couldn't understand why someone would carry it out in such a roundabout fashion. By the morning, I had a long list of possibilities, but I had no way of eliminating any of them without gathering further data. So I set out in the early hours of the morning to gather what information I could.

As I walked out into the fields, I met a young shepherd boy, not more than ten or twelve, who was more than willing to give me details of the incident and to show me the place where the dead animals had been found. I examined the area as meticulously as I could, given that it has been several days since the occurrence. He told me it had been a mate of his who had found them early one morning, and the local police had been quick to act, removing the carcasses to a slaughterhouse in Moreton. The police had made a rudimentary inquiry, interviewing the boy who found the sheep and the owner, a Mr Parker, but since then there has been no sight of any police activity in the village. My next step was to make a call at this Parker fellow. He is one of the wealthiest farmers in the Cotswolds, from what I gather, and his farm is made up of a cluster of large buildings located in an isolated part of the area. It took me a couple of hours to get there, and approaching the farmstead was a most forbidding experience. The area is desolate and unpeopled. The farm must employ at least twenty or thirty people, but I didn't encounter a soul as I walked down the road and up to the main building. A footman let me in, however, and I was soon sitting on a comfortable sofa with a cup of coffee in my lap.

Reginald Parker is a portly man in his late fifties who tries to act like a normal man, but cannot quite hide the fact that he is an eccentric, and who is more interested in petting and feeding his little lapdog than he is in talking to people or pretending to like receiving visitors to his home. From what I understand, he is an astute businessman. His answers to my questions were short and did not amount to much, but what I managed to find out was that he is the largest sheep farmer in all of Gloucestershire, and that he inherited the business from his father, deceased these four years. He is wealthy, and his farm is making much money, which makes him vulnerable to speculators and livestock thieves, but when I asked him whether he had recently turned down a protection racket or an offer to sell his business, he indicated quite clearly that such phenomena were remote to his world. He may have been lying, but if so, out of fear rather than malice. He is a strange man, to be sure, and his taste in decoration indicates that he has travelled, but there is so much affectation about him that it's hard to tell what is real and what is artifice.

I left his farm only a quarter of an hour after I had arrived, and started to walk back to the village to try and find you. The fog was growing thicker and a slight drizzle began. I was halfway across the valley when I heard a piercing howl, similar to that of a wolf or a hound. It was followed by a scream, and I immediately set off in the direction of the sound. After running for a few minutes, I came upon the little gorge where Dalton was lying. There was no sign of anyone else, but I could hear voices, so I hid behind a little bush and watched what happened. Three shepherds came running, and they went up to the body, arguing among themselves. Having made sure he was dead, they decided to go and fetch help and so they all went away again. This gave me enough time to carry out a full investigation of the scene before you all came back to trample all over the place."

Holmes took a big puff of smoke on his pipe and leaned back in his chair. I had been listening with great interest, but felt there was more to tell.

"Are you sure you told us everything you managed to infer from investigating the crime scene? I had a feeling you were withholding some things that you didn't want to disclose in front of everyone."

"There is nothing conclusive. Except that in this envelope…" He produced a small white envelope folded in half out of his inner pocket. "…I have the ashes from one of the cigarettes that had been smoked at the scene of the murder. I thought it necessary to salvage, as it is quite an unusual type of tobacco. Slovenian, if I'm not mistaken. So when we find a man who smokes Slovenian cigarettes, we are close to the solution!"

"Well, that shouldn't be too difficult in this part of the world."

"Don't be so sure, Watson. There are more immigrants in this country than one might think. They are quite apt at avoiding the law, and one might very conceivably stumble upon a family of Mongolians in the cellar of a vicarage."

"Anything else?"

"Not really. Only that there were quite a lot of handprints in the mud along with the footprints."

"Made by Dalton presumably, when he was thrown to the ground by the attack?"

"Yes, but he was attacked from the front not from behind, which would make him fall on his back."

I threw my hands up in resignation.

"What are we to make of all this? Slovenian cigarettes, a rusty fork, and a murder that seems to be the work of some wild animal the likes of which these islands have never seen!"

"My view of it is not quite as gloomy as yours."

"But half of the village seems to think this has a supernatural explanation! I told you about the incident at church. They believe it is the doing of some devilish wolf. A werewolf!"

"Poppycock, Watson!"

"You should look into the history of this place, Holmes. Colonel Draycot told me that several men here were accused of being werewolves during the witch hunts."

"Which did happen three hundred years ago. But you interest me, Watson. The way the simple folk try to understand things to which they are unable to provide a natural explanation can be quite revealing. Shepherding is one of the world's oldest occupations, and since time immemorial it has been connected to man's chronic fear of the wolf. Wolves roamed this land once, too, and maybe the myth of the wolf, or, indeed, of the werewolf, lives on since then, in the subconscious layers of people's minds."

"But do you not think it is possible that a wolf, or some other vicious animal, has escaped from some menagerie, or even, by some unlikely accident, managed to cross the channel from the continent?"

"You saw the wounds on that poor man, Watson. What does your medical knowledge tell you?"

"Well, as I said, I have enough experience of tiger injuries to say it was not a tiger."

"A reasonable observation, given that we are in Gloucestershire."

"No, if it was an animal, it was a larger animal."

"And a wolf is not larger than a tiger."

"No, but a bear is."

"Quite true, but bears are almost as foreign to these lands as tigers. More foreign, I should think, since I have reason to believe that many people who come back from the colony bring tiger cubs with them."

"But if an exotic animal can be brought to this country by a human, can it not be just about any wild animal on the planet? Or at least one that is indigenous to a British colony, which hardly narrows down the options."

"Yes, it is possible. But that would mean ignoring the howl that I heard."

"Oh yes, I forgot about that. Are you sure it was a wolf's howl?"

"No, it could also have been..." Holmes smiled. "...a gigantic hound..."

I smiled back.

"There is another possibility."

"What's that?"

"It could have been the boom of the bittern."

We both laughed.

"We have been in similar situations before, have we not, my dear fellow?" Holmes clapped his hands. "But the lesson we learned then is that we should consider the most likely possibilities first."

"And what is the most likely?"

"That this has been carried out by a human, making it look like the work of an animal or even a monster, in order to disguise the deed."

"Would it not be wiser to disguise it into something more probable?"

"Obviously. Which should make us wonder if this disguise is not probable to the people in this region, or some of them."

"You mean someone wants to scare them?"

"Yes. The question is, scare them into what?"

Holmes stroked his lips with his forefinger.

"What do you think?" I asked.

"I think we should tread carefully. We are strangers here, after all. My experience tells me that we should start by looking into the victim rather than the offender. Why should Rover Dalton be murdered?"

"You hardly suggest we go and talk to his poor family, do you?"

"No. I suggest we go where a working man's true self may be found."

"And where might that be?"

"Didn't you talk about a tavern at the other edge of the valley? I'm sure Rover Dalton spent more time there than with his family, like every true Englishman."

And so we ventured out into the cold evening air to visit the little inn I had stumbled upon on my walk the day before. It was getting dark quite fast now, and I had not been prepared to interrupt the comfortable sejour in front of the fireplace, but Holmes' enthusiasm made me hopeful of his mental state, and it rubbed off on me. The Green Man catered to a different class of people than Mrs. Faversham's inn, a fact that I had not reflected upon on my previous visit. When we stepped in, the interior appeared quite different than I remembered, much due to it being filled with loud and mud-spattered shepherds and farmhands on their day off. After a few minutes, I realised that these men were in their Sunday clothes, black suits in contrast to the hard-wearing tweed and fustian of their workday dress, but on their feet were boots and wellingtons covered in mud, telling of long walks across field and fen to get to the luring hearth of their local.

The landlord recognised me, and was the first person to smile at us as we had entered. We each ordered a pint of cider, and the landlord introduced us to the assembly of men at the counter. One of them was the old farmer I had met earlier at the vicar's luncheon party, the old man who had identified the sheep killings as the work of a wild boar. His name was Brody, and he inspected us with a sceptical gaze. Next to him was one of the young shepherds who had shown us to the murder site, a skinny boy, not older than twenty, called Pointer. From what I could gather, he was employed at Mr Brody's farm.

"Word has it," said Brody, "that you've been to see Mr Parker."

Holmes seemed slightly surprised by his knowledge.

"I see it's true what they say about the countryside, that news travels fast here."

Brody smiled, revealing several non-existent teeth.

"The countryside may appear desolate, but there is always someone watching."

"That is an interesting point."

Brody took a large gulp from his pot of beer.

"Very few people ever take the trouble to go up to Mr Parker's place, let alone to visit Parker himself. If you've any business at his farm, it very seldom involves speaking to the man himself."

"He is a curious man. Quite unlike any farmer I have met."

"Ah, 'tis the result of success. Reach a certain point, an' it goes to yer head."

"Has he always been such a character?" I asked.

"Naah, maybe four or five years. It was the death of his wife that finally pushed him over the edge."

"He didn't seem a madman to me, Mr Brody," Holmes remarked. "An eccentric, perhaps, but no more than that."

"Ah, you know how it is, Mr Holmes." This was the landlord butting in. "When a man keeps to himself like that, people begin to talk."

"Really? And what do they say?"

The landlord smiled.

"That he's a madman."

Holmes laughed.

"But if it's rumour you want," said Brody, "you should look into His Lordship."

"His Lordship?"

"See, this here region, it's all sheep farming. And it's doing good business these days, despite some problems with sheep liver rot and new legislations concerning tenant rights.

But Parker has created a little niche of his own. Years ago, he was just a tenant farmer, like all the rest of us, but then he managed to strike a deal with the lord of the manor which allowed him to make a larger profit from his farming without increasing the lord's share. This made it possible for Parker to buy land from the surrounding tenants, and now he dominates the local sheep farming business completely. At the same time, the other farmers under Upper Slaughter Manor are struggling to make ends meet. The lord of the manor, meanwhile, has cut himself off from the farming that goes on on his land, and he doesn't seem to care that his tenancy is unfair or that he could make a much larger profit from Parker's business."

Holmes' eyes were fixed on Brody, his concentration absolute.

"So to all intents and purposes," I said, "Parker rules the area while the squire has his mind elsewhere?"

"That's about the size of it."

"And what's the name of this lord of the manor?"

"His name is Gilbert Slaughter."

"You do know, of course," said the landlord, "that the name of the lord and the village has nothing to do with the word 'slaughter'. It comes from the old English word *slohtre*, which simply means 'muddy place'." He smiled again.

"That may not be the meaning of it originally," said Brody, "but this area more than lives up to its name."

"Are you referring to the sheep slayings and Rover Dalton?" I probed.

"That is nothing more than a rekindlin' of the curse that has been set on this place several centuries back."

"I'm sure the gentlemen have heard the old witchcraft stories," said the landlord.

"Aye, but are they aware that it has a basis in truth? The witch hunters went about listening to the local folklore and the people of the village were wont to tell the truth to men of authority. What they heard were a lot of old wives' tales and ghost stories that they turned into concrete suspicions that suited their own purposes. But in every cottage that they visited, one story was told repeatedly, and with a passion that was unmatched by the other tales. And that was the tale of the creature."

"Ah," said Holmes, appearing quite disappointed by this twist. "And what sort of creature might this be?"

"Well, when people retell it today, they tend to describe it as a werewolf. But werewolves are not indigenous to this country. I would say that originally, the tale was of some other, more elusive creature."

"Such as…?"

Brody slowly put down his tankard on the counter.

"The tales all describe it as a great hairy thing, with a horrible face, great fangs and clawed paws."

"Do they? How inventive of them."

"I'm not saying that's what's responsible for the recent deaths, Mr Holmes, but it is uncanny, is it not, how it all adds up?"

"But this would mean that this monster, apart from being a supernatural being, defies the laws of nature also by being about four hundred years old."

"The lords of the manor have always been werewolves."

This was Pointer, the young man, who had suddenly entered into the conversation.

"Do you know that for a fact?" asked Holmes.

"It's what my old man used to say. He used to work as a handyman up at the manor house. When there was a full moon, His Lordship would lock himself into a remote part of the house and terrible sounds could be heard all night. That was when the old squire was lord. He's dead now, but his son has inherited his curse, just like he inherited it from his father, and there have been werewolves in Upper Slaughter all since the Middle Ages."

I couldn't help but let out a small snicker at this, but Holmes looked serious.

"It is an interesting theory, Mr Pointer. Commendable in that it seems to explain all the important points of the mystery at hand."

Was he joking? I slowly realised that he was not. In spite of his adherence to the ideal of logic reasoning, Holmes' goal was always to look for the most likely hypothesis, no matter how incredible it sounded. So if a theory explained what needed to be explained, then that was the one to pursue. It had to be proved first, of course. Holmes took a sip of his beer, then slammed the pot onto the counter.

"Well, gentlemen, this is all very thought-provoking, but what we really came for was information about the deceased, Dalton. Did any of you know him?"

"I did," said Pointer. "Or at least I worked with him. He was a difficult man to get to know, was Rover. Didn't do much talking. They say he came back from India that way. That he was quite a different sort of man before he went."

"Do you know where he was posted?" I asked.

Pointer and Brody looked at each other.

"India," said Pointer.

"Yes, but what part of India?"

"India has parts?" said Brody.

"All right, then, what division did he belong to? Was he an artillery man?"

"I couldn't say, sir," said Pointer. "But he did see some action over there."

"When did he come back?"

"About three years ago."

I was puzzled.

"There hasn't been any fighting over there for years. Was he present at the rebellion? Or was he a campaigner, perhaps, like me?"

"Campaigner?"

"Did he fight in Afghanistan?"

"That was years ago, wasn't it?" said the landlord. "Dalton only went to India about six or seven years ago."

"Then he can't have taken part in any battles, unless he was witness to something else that had a lasting impression upon him."

"He never talked about it to anyone," Pointer insisted.

"What about his wife?" asked Holmes.

"Least of all her. It was well-known that, as far as she was concerned, her husband never came back from India. She and their boys led their own life. Rover brought in the money, but little else."

"Sounds like a dismal fellow to have as your workmate," I commented.

Pointer looked me straight in the eyes for the first time.

"He was the best shepherd ever to work in the Cotswolds. It was an honour to work alongside him."

"I have no doubt," I was quick to remark.

These men and their curious internal relationships were a mystery to me, like similar relationships I had encountered before. They seemed to me not dissimilar to those of private soldiers, or to police constables, retaining a sort of mutual respect and solidarity that would turn into hostility as soon as an outsider stepped into their realm. I have seen privates joking among themselves in barracks, their smiles turning into stone faces within seconds of an officer entering the room.

Holmes discreetly signalled to me that our work here was done. I could think of a dozen more questions to pose to these men, but I also realised that we should not risk them closing up like clams by being too inquisitive, and so we drank the last of our cider and politely took our leave. We had barely stepped out through the door, however, before Holmes drew a loud breath of relief.

"Strewth!" he exclaimed. "I will never get accustomed to the subdued ways of country folk. Did you see the look Brody gave you when you said you were an old campaigner? I don't think he has anything against soldiers, but when an outsider heralds allegiance to anything foreign, I'm sure he looks upon it with suspicion, no matter what it is. But where a cockney would punch you in the eye for being strange, a peasant only serves you with that murderous inscrutable gaze. Oh, if only this was a case of murder in London! This place makes me long for opium-stinking lascars and smart-talking cabbies."

"Shall we pack it in and go home, then?"

"Oh my dear fellow, I wouldn't miss this case for the world! I am quite delighted that you brought me here."

"That's not what you said when we first came here."

"Are we going to have that discussion again?"

I fell silent, and we walked a few paces, leaving the cluster of houses behind us. But then I changed my mind.

"Yes, dammit! We *are* going to have this discussion again, and we will keep having it until you realise…"

"Realise what?"

Holmes stopped and turned towards me, his face indicating that his question was sincere. I didn't quite know how to answer him, though.

"Well…"

"Realise what, Watson?"

"That you are unreasonable!"

"Unreasonable?"

"Unreasonable."

"Are you sure you have the right word?"

"Quite sure. Why wouldn't I?"

"Watson, if I'm not a man of reason, then what am I?"

I continued walking.

"You are not as reasonable as you think you are. In some parts, perhaps, yes, very reasonable indeed, but in others you are a slave to your whims and emotions."

"Watson, this is a side to you that I haven't encountered before in our relationship. From whence does it come?"

"You can't pretend to be an easy man to live with."

"No, no, I am well aware of that. But I always thought you accepted that as a fact."

"Well, perhaps I have grown fond enough of you to the degree that I want to help you."

This time, it was Holmes' turn to stop walking.

"You know full well that I am beyond help. Besides, I don't want help."

"Well, I suppose I have allowed myself to be influenced by you, trying to solve every problem that comes my way."

"There is a great difference between a problem that wants to be solved and one that does not."

"I'm not so sure *this* problem wants to be solved."

"What makes you say that?"

"I don't know. A shepherd who was well respected, yes, but friend to no one, and distant to his wife and family. And the villagers seem to have cared more about the loss of the capital that is a flock of sheep than the violent death of a man. I can't even see why anyone would take the trouble of killing him. I mean, saying he was murdered because he had seen something and needed to be silenced, I don't think he was the type of man to share what he had seen with anybody."

"This is interesting, Watson. You really have developed quite a remarkable talent for stimulating speculations."

"I realise that they are speculations, but what do we have to base our reasoning on?"

"Quite a lot, I'd say."

"Really? What?"

"Do you see, Watson? This problem *did* want solving, after all!"

He laughed heartily, and I couldn't help but be infected, and soon we were laughing to our hearts' content. As the sound trailed off, however, it was succeeded by a distant howl. The buildings were well behind us by now, and we had entered a small copse that bordered onto the fields where sheep grazed in the daytime. This is where the howl had come from.

"What on earth is that?" I asked.

"Boom of the bittern, d'you think?" Holmes winked at me, and managed to relieve a bit of my initial anxiety. "Let's take a look."

Before he had finished that sentence, he was off, dashing in through the trees like a dog on the scent. I quickly followed suit, but had trouble keeping up with Holmes, being cruelly reminded of a haunting jezail bullet. Holmes stopped abruptly behind a tree trunk, and turned towards me. His eyes were wide open. My ear was reached by the sound of snarling, growing rapidly louder within a second, until it made me turn around. It passed me only a few feet away, a great black or dark grey apparition, running on all fours, galloping like a hare. It ran past Holmes and then disappeared again behind a row of thick bushes. The moment from when it first appeared until it vanished again had been no more than two or three seconds.

"Did you see it, Watson!"

"What on earth was that?"

"The answer to all our questions." Holmes turned from me again, and ran towards the bushes. I followed behind, and could hear him breaking twigs and scampering through piles of leaves. Then I heard him moan loudly to himself, and he shouted back to me: "It's gone! We lost it!" I waited at the edge of the shrubbery, and within seconds Holmes came out of it.

"The question is," he said, "what will it accomplish this time?"

IV. A Grotesque Interlude

The sighting of the curious and impalpable beast in the forest left me shaken and uneasy. Holmes and I had encountered many mysterious things before this, and were to encounter many more, but never before had I been startled by such an ungodly thing, horrible in its great size and rapidity. Even afterwards, I was not quite sure what it was I had seen, and even though I knew that it was a creature unlike anything I had hitherto witnessed, I was unwilling to yield to such a notion, trying to convince myself that I had not really seen anything. If truth be told, the whole incident had passed so quickly I was not quite sure what I saw, but the unease and the horror that I felt when it happened, the memory of which remained in me for some time afterwards, was an unavoidable indication that what I wished I hadn't seen was exactly what I had seen.

Holmes and I returned to the village, which lay quiet in the dimness of the evening. There was no stir, and no indication that the creature we had seen had caused any unrest. We walked back to the inn, where Mrs. Faversham was waiting anxiously for us, telling us that we had missed supper, but that there were some cold leftovers for us. I gladly accepted the offer, but Holmes rushed right past us and up the stairs, his poor manners courtesy of enthusiasm and anticipation rather than a bad mood. The landlady and I heard him slam his door shut above us, and I escorted the lady into the parlour telling her not to worry, this was the run of the mill with Mr Holmes.

The next morning I was awakened by bright sunlight, and the gloom and terror of the previous day seemed to me a strange but distant fantasy. Upon leaving my room to go down to breakfast, I passed Holmes' door. Curiosity induced me to lean down and peep in through his keyhole. The room appeared dark, the curtains probably drawn, as Holmes abhorred sunlight. I could not see Holmes, or say whether he was up or not, but when my face came close to the keyhole, the pungent odour of tobacco smoke reached my nose, and I even fancied I could see thin veils of smoke coming out, tell-tale signs that Holmes had been up early, or all night, engaging in a deep mediation concerning the problem at hand. I couldn't wait to hear what conclusions he would make. I went down to breakfast, and took small helpings from the buffet so as to draw out the process, allowing time for Holmes to finish his doings upstairs and come down to join me. I helped myself to a local newspaper, and then another, as I had my second course of scrambled eggs, but after an hour and a half, Holmes had still not appeared, and I grew restless. Mrs. Faversham interrupted my protracted ritual by giving me a small envelope. It contained a dinner invitation for Holmes and me from Mr and Mrs. Tibbins that very evening, and I told the landlady to give an affirmative reply to the message boy waiting outside.

As I folded up my copy of the Cirencester Herald, I was reached by the sound of commotion from the street outside. I arose from the breakfast table and cast a glance out of the window. There was a large carriage coming down the main street, and it was followed by a crowd of people gathering from the adjacent houses and alleys. It stopped right in front of the inn, and out of it came a policeman in uniform and an old man in a greatcoat carrying a Gladstone bag. I surmised that it was a man from the Gloucestershire Constabulary and a local pathologist who had come to make investigations into the death of Dalton. They were greeted by Mr Tibbins and Colonel Draycot, who seemed to be the official representative of the village in matters like these.

I assumed that Holmes would be interested in whatever this inquiry came up with, and so quickly stepped out of the dining room and went up to tell my companion of the news. I knocked on his door and was immediately asked to step in. Holmes was sitting at the table by the window, leaning forward. When I was beside him, he looked up and smiled.

"Good morning, Watson. I trust you had a good breakfast?"

I couldn't help but notice that the thing on the table with which he had been so consumed was the rusty fork that he had found at the scene of the murder. He saw that my gaze was directed towards it, and leaned back in his chair.

"Interesting, wouldn't you say?"

"Whatever can it mean?"

"I must confess, I have no comprehensible conclusions." He picked it up very carefully, as if it was a precious archaeological find. "So far, I can only infer that it is very old. At least a couple of hundred years, if not more."

"Really? How can you tell?"

He held it up to the light.

"If you try to look beyond the deformity it has acquired from the rust, you can see that it is quite a decorative thing, and much bigger than the table forks we use today. You know, a few centuries ago, the fork was quite rare as a utensil when eating food. It wasn't until the eighteenth century that it was commonly used in the way it is now. And you can see from the size and shape that this was not intended as a table fork."

"But if it's that old, then it's quite possible it has nothing to do with the murder. It could have been dropped there ages ago!"

"It's quite possible. But that would be a coincidence the improbability of which deserves investigating."

I hurried to tell him about the arrival of the policeman and the pathologist, since I thought we should get going before we missed anything. But Holmes didn't take his eyes from the fork.

"Yes, I'm sure they will do a good job without our assistance."

"But are you not curious to find out what results they will arrive at?"

"Whatever it is, it's bound to be something dull."

"And the post mortem, don't you want to know what it reveals?"

"I know what it will reveal. That Dalton was killed by a savage blow to his head by a blunt instrument and that he was fit as a fiddle in all other respects."

"Come now, Holmes, you cannot be so sure of that! It could show anything! That he had some rare disease…"

"That caused his skull to cave in? Yes, it's possible, but highly unlikely."

"Well, not that caused his death, but something that tells us about who he was."

"That will surely become apparent at the inquest tomorrow. But if you are so eager to go and have a look, please do so. I will concentrate my attention to this fork, and see if I can't hunt down some chemicals to do some tests on it."

I left Holmes to his investigations, and went off on my own. As I stepped out in the street, I could see the entourage of people disappearing into the open doors of the village hall. The hall was a large whitewashed building with a neoclassical façade which made up one side of a triangular village square at the farther end of the main street. Coming in through the doors, I mingled with the rest of the crowd, hoping to catch something of the investigators' conversation, or at least snap up a piece of gossip from the other onlookers. The policeman was introduced as Superintendent Ferrett of the Gloucestershire Constabulary and the pathologist was a Dr Stanley Collins. They were shown in through a door that seemed to lead down to a cellar where I guessed the corpse was kept. The public was held back by a couple of large guards, and the door was closed.

Among the curious men that started to walk back out of the building with a disgruntled appearance, I could see young Mr Pointer from last night, accompanied by a couple of other men of the same age. I stepped up to them and greeted Pointer politely. The sneering laughter that was on his and his friends' faces faded away swiftly, and was replaced by the sheepish countenance that he had displayed the night before.

"Oh, Mr Watson, sir."

The other boys greeted me by grasping the front of their caps.

"Seems like this business will be cleared up shortly," I said, trying to start a conversation.

"What does the police care about a dead shepherd?" said one of the boys, a young man with a flat blonde fringe exposed below his close-fitting cricket cap. "They'll only do as much as they are required to and then leave it. We won't see those men again."

"Well," I laughed, "I am the first to admit that the police's methods are not always the most fruitful, but surely they will pursue the matter?"

"They did nothing when Polly Barnett was kicked in the stomach by her husband, causing her to miscarriage. They did nothing to find the culprit when someone set fire to old Mr Whitby's haybarn."

I was being given a glimpse of what the daily lives of these poor peasants looked like, and started to regret having initiated this exchange, but I told myself their words could be revealing, so persisted.

"So the long arm of the law doesn't quite reach all the way to Upper Slaughter, does it?"

"You can say that again!" corroborated the blonde fringed boy.

"It's quite a hard life for all us shepherds," said Pointer. "And now it's a dangerous life, too."

"Are you afraid after what happened to Dalton?"

"Damn right we're afraid," said the third young man, whose face was covered with a patchy black beard that made it look dirty. "Little Gerald, the Gilchrists' lad, heard the wolf howl the other night, and ran all the way back to his parents' farm, four miles it was, leaving his flock out there for the beast to take!"

"And did it?"

"No, he was lucky. An older farmhand came along and took care of it."

"And then there are these bleedin' gypsies." This was blonde fringe talking again. "They go round the countryside, setting up camp in remote groves of trees carrying out their heretic rituals."

"Nah, there are no gypsies in this part of the land," said patchy beard. "You're thinking about the carnival. Now there's a charismatic lot! They've got a bearded lady an' all. Wouldn't surprise me if they had a monster in a rusty cage too!"

"They'll want to check the lock of that cage," joked Pointer and they laughed.

I wondered to myself how much of what they told me was based on first-hand experience and how much of it was local folklore. Gypsies have roamed the land for centuries,

65

but to my knowledge they have always been much more harmless than popular opinion claims. However, if there were gypsies in the vicinity, I thought, they might know more about this business than many others. Travelling carnivals seemed to me a rare thing in this part of the country, although I was well aware that they were skilled in avoiding contact with the law, and their talent for navigating the land without moving on the main roads made them difficult to monitor.

We remained outside the village hall together with a few other curious men and women for a good half hour, waiting for the investigators to come out again and maybe give us a few clues as to what they had come up with, but gradually I grew restless, and realised that they were carrying out a post mortem in there, which would take quite a long time. I started to think that Holmes had been correct, and that the wisest thing to do was wait for the inquest, when all would be revealed. Then suddenly the door to the village hall sprung open, and one of the guards came out. He was a big sturdy fellow, and he walked straight towards me.

"Is your name Watson?" he said in an indifferent voice.

"How did you guess?" I asked with a smile, then looked around and realised that everyone else was quite obviously a rural labourer.

"You're wanted inside," the guard said, and turned around and started to walk back, taking it for granted that I would follow him.

I did follow him, overtaken by curiosity, and I was led in and walked down stairs to a cold and murky cellar, where, in a large undecorated chamber, three men were assembled around a primitive wooden table. Approaching this table, I could see that upon it lay the disembowelled body of Rover Dalton, as if he was just a piece of surplus meat stowed away in a storage room. The men looked at me with bored faces, and the pathologist, whose white apron was covered in blood, raised his eyebrows.

"Ah, Dr Watson! I was told you were in the vicinity, and I could use another opinion from a medical man."

I stopped halfway across the floor, reluctant to go up to the others uninvited.

"If I can be of assistance."

"You can! Come up to the body and let us know your opinion on what you see."

I continued my walk through the vast room, and as I moved closer, the row of men, made up of various dignitaries from the region, parted and allowed me to step up to the table. What I saw was both horrible and strange. Dalton's abdomen had been expertly sliced open, revealing the contents of his stomach. They were made up of three small objects, each the size of an apple, and when I looked closer I could identify them as three baby rabbits, well-developed and covered with a thin wet fur, but still so young that they could well be mere foetuses a week or so from birth.

"What in…?" I was lost for words. I raised my head and looked at the other men, my gaze finally landing on the pathologist.

"Tell me, Doctor," he said. "Have you ever encountered anything like this?"

"Absolutely not," I said.

"Do you have any reasonable explanation for it?"

I looked at the little rabbits once more. They were all curled up as if they had crept inside this man's stomach for the night, just as they would creep into a burrow.

"Well…" I reasoned that my only option was do my thinking out loud. "He could hardly have swallowed them whole. And yet, they are completely intact and do not show signs of having been chewed." Listening to my own words, they sounded absurd. "Er, could they have crept inside the body after it was dead?"

"That would mean crawling through the oesophagus," replied the pathologist. "Quite impossible for a baby rabbit, since they are born blind and barely able to move."

"And yet they look unborn, as if he was carrying them."

"Which, of course, is the most unlikely explanation of all these unlikely explanations."

"Incredible explanations, I would say."

The pathologist put his hands on the table and lowered his head towards the floor for a couple of moments.

"Then your professional opinion, Dr Watson, is that this phenomenon is unknown to science and possibly also unexplainable through current scientific knowledge?"

"Well, yes…"

"I would like that put to the record," said the pathologist to a man next to him, who replied by scribbling on a notepad. "Thank you, Dr Watson. We can carry on without your assistance."

I felt the urge to tell Holmes at once about my strange experience. I found him in the sitting room, with a cup of coffee on the sideboard and a book in his lap. He seemed delighted to see me, and I sat down impatiently, telling him the whole story, from my being summoned by the guard to the pathologist dismissing me. His face reflected both amusement and puzzlement in reaction to my narrative. When I had finished, he was quiet for a while, a faint smile on his lips betraying a perverse contentment at being furnished with the most ideal food for thought imaginable.

"How singular," he said finally.

"Is that all you have to say?" I remarked.

"Well, what you have just told me certainly defies all attempts at verbal response. I do not think I have ever heard anything quite like it."

"And what do you make of it?"

"Nothing much. It is precarious to theorise without sufficient data."

"But how would you account for it? Is there any explanation for it?"

"No natural one that I can think of."

"Then you lean towards a supernatural explanation? Witchcraft, for instance?"

Holmes raised his hands slightly.

"My dear friend, let us wait before we use such extravagant words. Leave the sensational aspects of this business aside for a moment, difficult though it may be, and instead ask yourself this: Why do you think you were called for to inspect the body?"

"To corroborate the pathologist's assessment of course."

"And don't you think the pathologist was competent enough to conclude that it was unnatural for a grown man to have three unborn rabbits in his stomach?"

"Well yes, but the poor man was dumbfounded! He probably just needed someone to confirm to him that he wasn't dreaming!"

"And the other men in the room couldn't do that?"

"They were not medical men. He was longing for the assistance of someone with a similar education."

"Who were the other men?"

"I didn't recognise them. It was a stout and well-dressed man who had the appearance of a gentleman, and a more robust-looking fellow, probably some sort of warden."

"Hm! And no policeman?"

"Yes, but he was waiting outside. It all seemed quite in order to me. What are your suspicions?"

"Nothing, Watson. Nothing. Take no notice of me."

And he returned to his little book. I observed that it was the clothbound volume that he had entertained himself with on our journey here a few days earlier, and I asked what it was. He held it up to me so that I could read the back, which said "The Golden Bough" in golden letters on a black background. I was about to ask him what it was about, but he immediately went back to reading, and looked so absorbed and peaceful that I decided to leave him.

V. The Wild Man

That same evening, we departed for the vicarage and our dinner with the Tibbinses. Holmes appeared greatly invigorated by the meditations to which he had devoted his day, and there was no sign of the languor which had so paralysed him a few days before. This change in demeanour delighted me, of course, but knowing that he could so easily fall back into melancholy made for a relentless apprehension at the back of my head. However, so long as the mystery in hand continued to deliver strange and unexpected turns, I had no reason to fear for Holmes' mental health. His physical health was another matter.

We were greeted at the door by Mrs. Tibbins, who had neither the ability nor the will to hide her excitement at having us (and by "us" I mean Holmes) as dinner guests. We had hardly stepped over the threshold before she started asking him questions. I expected him to react with embarrassment and maybe ask her to calm down and be patient, but to my great surprise he indulged her overexcitement. He answered her questions with a similar giddiness as he took her hand and was led inside as if an old female acquaintance of our hostess. To my delight, her husband kindly escorted me through the door and into the parlour, where we were served some invigorating red wine. Mrs. Tibbins continued asking Holmes about his methods and his most famous cases, about which she had read profusely and could remember even minute details, which gave me the suspicion that she had reread them in preparation for this meeting. The vicar and I commenced our own discussion on mundane topics, including the weather in this part of the country, and what type of footwear proved most practical in the local terrain.

It wasn't until we were halfway through the main course of dinner that conversation turned to the grisly events of the recent days.

"Any progress, Mr Holmes?" queried the vicar.

Holmes looked secretive, but could not hide a discreet smile.

"At this point in an investigation," he said, "we are in a world of theories, but with no sufficient evidence to verify any of them."

The Tibbinses looked eagerly at each other, waiting for Holmes to continue. But he did not.

"Holmes generally prefers to air verified inferences rather than speculative theories," I explained. "It is one of his methods of making other people feel inferior to him."

I winked at Holmes and he winked back.

"What I can say, however," he continued, "is that there are a number of promising clues. I would almost venture to say that there are too many clues!"

"Too many clues?" said Mr Tibbins. "What does that mean?"

"That someone has planted clues in order to lead us in a certain direction, maybe?" I said.

"Yes," replied Holmes slowly. "Or to warn us from moving in a certain direction."

Tibbins leaned across the dinner table and held out his hands.

"But what I can't seem to grasp is why anyone should want to murder poor Dalton. If we establish a likely motive, then that might be a good starting point."

"But as you say yourself, my good vicar, the motive is completely obscure, and we have practically no clues to it. No no, motive is boring. What reasons do people have for murdering other people? Money? Jealousy? The most vulgar and commonplace impulses of our species. There is almost no variation to the patterns of murder motives, which demonstrates quite clearly what base animals we humans are. But what separates us from the animals is our creativity, and the curious ways in which we go about our business. That is where my interest lies, and that, to me, is the most fruitful point of departure."

"And how was Dalton murdered, then?"

Holmes shrugged.

"I believe we all agree that he was set upon by some vicious beast, possibly one unknown to science."

"Surely you don't believe that, Mr Holmes," said Mrs. Tibbins with a laugh.

"You have medical qualifications yourself. How else would you account for Dalton's injuries?"

"Well, his head injury could have been inflicted by just about anything, for a start. And the wounds on his chest, well, scratches like that are easy to replicate. Maybe with some garden tool or a pitchfork."

"A pitchfork, you say? That's interesting. Yes, we must not forget that we are dealing with farmers, and that means we must consider specific methods available and specific ways of thinking. Local folklore tells of a werewolf haunting these parts, I believe?"

"Not a werewolf," protested the vicar. "That is simply how it was reinterpreted by the witch hunters. What they accommodated to suit their own ends was a legend of a monster haunting the surrounding forests."

"Forests?" I countered. "What forests?"

The vicar smiled patiently.

"Yes, it seems unlikely today, but no more than three or four hundred years ago, this part of the country had quite a lot of woodlands."

"And what of the lords of the manor," I said, "and the werewolf curse that lies upon them?"

"Ah, I see you have been talking to the locals. No, that too is a later version, probably stimulated by a growing displeasure with the lords and how they have distributed their tenancies."

"You are acquainted with Lord Slaughter?" inquired Holmes.

The vicar shifted uneasily in his seat.

"I wouldn't say that."

"Whatever you've heard about him, apart from the werewolf rumours, is probably true!" his wife filled in. "He does not encourage visitors."

"What we fail to see nowadays," the vicar continued, "is that the aristocracy plays a very marginal role in ancient folklore, and is virtually non-existent in the tales of the creature."

Holmes and I shared a discreet glance, both noticing how the vicar had changed the subject.

"What sort of creature was it?" asked Holmes, accepting this turn in the conversation.

The vicar's smile returned.

"The accounts generally describe something in-between a man, a bear and a wolf, suggesting that the tale dates back to pagan times, when it is possible that both bears and wolves roamed this country."

"But since this is sheep farming country," I said, "is it not logical that the legend tells of a werewolf. Man's fear of the wolf has deep connections to their danger in relation to sheep farming."

"That's true. Which is probably also a reason why it changed into a werewolf legend as this area turned into a sheep herding area."

Holmes had listened with interest to the vicar's folkloric lecture, but his expression had all the time been one of mild amusement.

"This is all very interesting," he now said, "but local tales of unknown creatures always have one fallacy, namely the fact that for the creature to exist through the ages when the tale has been told, it would have to be virtually immortal."

"Ah, Mr Holmes," said the vicar, "your intellectual powers do not disappoint. I have no stronger belief in this superstition than you do, but it is necessary for us to understand it in order for us to understand the locals, you see."

"There I agree with you. But do you really think the farmers here still believe in a lot of old whimsy? After all, they live in the same modern age as do we."

The vicar shook his head without a flicker of doubt in his face.

"You would be surprised, Mr Holmes. When I go around visiting them in their little cottages, I see good luck charms and rituals that could have come straight out of the brothers Grimm. There is an old woman who talks to the fairies, and every week the doctor in Moreton is visited by people who claim to suffer from elf shot."

"Ha!" Holmes clapped his hands. "How fascinating! Do you know, you remind me that such superstitions actually exist even in the heart of London. It is most common among the costermongers and the street sellers, who are always afraid that one of their competitors will put a curse on them and ruin their business. Many of them go around with a dozen or so lucky charms pinned onto their clothes. I met one man who carried a dried cow's heart pierced through with several long nails to protect him against evil."

"You see? Stepping into the modern age does not automatically mean leaving the past behind."

"Speaking of the supernatural," Holmes said, "Watson had quite a strange experience today that might interest you."

The Tibbinses looked at me with wide eyes, and I obediently recounted my visit to the post mortem and what I had seen there. I expected my story to stir up the couple's astonishment, but to my surprise they looked at each other with a concerned but knowing glance.

"What you saw, Dr Watson," said the vicar, "would not be so strange to a Cotswolds man. You see, that is what, according to legend, happened to one of the witch hunters who came here in the seventeenth century. The local witches became so enraged by his presence that they put a curse on him. He was found dead one morning and when they opened him up, that was exactly what they found."

"Good God!" I said. "But I didn't think there were real witches here."

"There weren't!" Tibbins replied. "It's just a story."

"A story that has now become reality!" I said. "I can hardly believe what I'm hearing."

"Well, as I said, the people here live in the past. Such a thing would not be as strange to them as it is to us."

Mrs. Tibbins, who had been rather quiet, fiddling with her dessert spoon, suddenly raised her head.

"I suppose the one who takes the price out here is old Hob!"

Her husband chuckled and took a sip of wine.

"Old Hob?" I repeated.

"He's our wild man," replied the woman proudly.

"Wild man? You mean a real wild man, like the ones in medieval paintings? With clothes made of leaves and twigs and a mossy beard? You told me yourself, vicar, that they only had a symbolic meaning, like the green men."

"Well, I don't know if those were my exact words," he said shyly.

"He is a hermit," Mrs. Tibbins continued. "He lives as far from civilisation as possible in this part of the country."

"Now, there are different types of hermits," her husband commented. "Some look and behave just like you and me."

"But not Hob," his wife said. "He both looks and acts the part!"

The vicar made an attempt to curb his wife's enthusiasm by speaking very softly.

"You know, in my role as vicar, I try to go out to my flock as much as possible, and the idea is that I should not be deterred by remoteness or poverty or hostility. Hob seems to have been put here only to test my resilience. No one knows his real name. Some of the locals give him food and clothes, and have done for a long time, since it is considered bad luck to deny a hermit alms. But he sees nobody. I have been there two or three times, and have spoken to him extensively on matters of religion and philosophy."

"So he does accept God?" I asked.

"He accepts *a* God. But his system of belief is entirely his own, and eccentric in the extreme. And he has a way of speaking which is not easy to understand, since his only conversation partner is himself."

"Where does he live?" Holmes asked.

"He lives in the valley that borders onto the next shire. The woods there are very thick and impregnable, and he has dug out a hill right in the middle of it and made it his home."

"These woods," continued Holmes. "Are they far from here?"

"Brigham Woods? A couple of miles, maybe. They are right on the edge of the domain of Upper Slaughter manor, not too far from Parker's place."

To our astonishment, Holmes quickly rose from his chair.

"I demand that you take us there immediately!"

"What?" the vicar said. "Now?"

"Holmes," I protested. "It's ten o'clock at night! It's pitch black out there! And we're dressed for dinner!"

"Which is exactly why we must hurry. We have not a moment to lose. Mr Tibbins, I noticed on our way here that there is quite a large stable connected to this building. Am I right in surmising that there are a number of horses there?"

"Mr Holmes, you're not suggesting we ride to Brigham Woods at this hour?"

"That is exactly what I am suggesting."

"But what's the hurry?"

"I can tell you that on the way there."

And with these words he stepped out of the room, leaving us no option but to follow him. Mrs. Tibbins was the first to do so.

"Well I, for one, trust Mr Holmes!" she said, and almost jumped out of her chair.

And so it was that the Tibbins' groom was instructed to prepare four horses for a late night ride, while Holmes and I returned to the inn to change into our tweeds. Within fifteen minutes, we stepped outside to be greeted by the Tibbinses on horseback holding the reins of two further animals puffing and neighing without seeming to mind that it was almost midnight. Off we went, first out of the village towards the fields where I had spent my first day walking. We crossed these pastures swiftly, passing the place where Rover Dalton had met his end, and continued southwards. During our ride, the vicar implored Holmes to explain to us the reason for our hurry.

"It's quite simple, reverend. A man who lives out here is in great danger of that which killed Dalton, but since he lives here, in the middle of the wilds, he must have witnessed things that no one else here would have the opportunity to see. Therefore it is crucial that we get a chance to hear his story before it's too late!"

None of us had any reason to oppose Holmes' explanation, and the ride continued in silence. As we moved further from the pastures in the immediate surroundings of the village, the open fields were increasingly scattered with gnarled oak trees, until they were crowding the land to the extent that the field had turned into a forest. We suddenly reached a steep slope, the land dropping so dramatically that we could see above the tree tops, and observed how a wide forested valley, probably surrounding some sort of stream, stretched out before us. The slope proved difficult for the horses, and after trying to force them down a few metres, we decided to dismount, since we were now only a short walk from the hermit's dwelling place. We were lucky to be still in the early days of autumn, with what remained of the bright summer evenings, but as we proceeded deeper into the woods, it very soon became so dark that we could barely see anything apart from the silhouettes of the tree tops outlined against the full moon. The Tibbinses had come prepared, though, and produced a pair of bull's-eye lanterns, which lit the path before us. We secured our horses to a couple of low branches, and the vicar led the way forward. We continued down into the valley, and after a while I could hear the sound of trickling water, indicating that we were near the stream running along the bottom. The vicar guided us through the undergrowth until he shone his light on something ahead of us that looked like a small grassy hill.

"I think this is it!" he said and turned towards us. "You know, I cannot help but think of the possible connection between the phenomenon of wild men and the legend of the werewolf. I am reminded of the famous woodcut by Lucas Cranach the elder, in which the werewolf is depicted as a man gone feral, with a wild stare and an unkempt beard."

"Please, reverend," Holmes implored, "we have no time for this! Let us continue."

"Quite right."

We rounded the hill, all the time guided by the lights from the bull's eyes, until we came to a low rounded opening in the hillside. In the darkness it could have been a boulder or a patch of naked soil, but as we came up to it, I saw that it was a hole, just large enough for a man to fit into it in a hunched position. The vicar was just about to guide us into it, when Holmes grabbed his forearm.

"Wait!"

He looked down. We followed his example, and Mrs. Tibbins obliged him by shining her light on the ground in front of the hole. It was a mess of mud and grass, but the light also revealed a few pools of what could only be blood.

"We are too late," Holmes said, and vanished into the hole in the hillside.

Before we had time to follow him, he re-emerged.

"I beg you, do not come in here. I must examine the scene of the murder and I require it to be as unmoved as possible!"

"You mean he is dead?" Tibbins exclaimed, sounding quite horrified.

"The place is empty," Holmes said, "but it shows signs of a violent struggle, and there is more blood inside. Hob appears to have been abducted, but I doubt that he has been taken alive."

With this, Holmes grabbed the vicar's lantern and went back into the hermitage. Mrs. Tibbins had begun a small investigation of her own, kneeling down on the ground in front of the entrance, not minding that the wet mud made large stains on her gown.

"The blood is quite recent," she said. "I should think it happened only a few minutes ago. Hullo, what's this?"

"Footprints?" asked Tibbins.

"Handprints," said his wife. "But they are very large."

Holmes came out from the hermitage once more. He stood in front of the entrance, and I could see from his face that he was hot on the scent.

"It cannot be far away," he said. "We shall hunt it!"

He set off into the forest, stooping with his lantern so as to be able to follow the traces on the ground.

"What trail are we following, Mr Holmes?" asked Mrs. Tibbins.

"The trail of blood," he replied. "Look at these linear patterns in the mud, which indicate that the hermit's body has been dragged."

"Holmes," I said. "You don't think it is possible that this Hob is involved in the crime somehow? I mean, a wild man with a beard and ragged clothes could possibly be mistaken for a werewolf by the fanciful locals."

"But not by me! Whatever we saw among the trees last night outside the tavern, it wasn't a wild man."

We were interrupted by the piercing sound of a wolf's howl, such as the one we had heard previously.

"Impossible!" said the vicar. "There are no wolves here."

"This is no wolf," said Holmes, and quickened his pace.

"What, then?" I said, and was extremely frustrated by his refusal to answer.

Holmes continued down the hill, but after a few metres he stopped abruptly, allowing us to catch up with him. He was shining his light in among the trees, and then he froze.

"There!" he said and pointed.

I strained to see what it was, but could only just discern something moving down by the stream. Holmes ran towards it, and I could see someone running to the left along the water, but Holmes stopped at the place from where the figure had set out. When we arrived there, we saw him stooped over the savaged body of an old man.

"Hob!" cried the vicar.

"Watson!" said Holmes. "You and Mrs. Tibbins must take care of the old man. There is still some life left in him. Don't let it leave him without hearing what he has to say!"

"Where are you going?"

"I'm going after the monster!"

With these words he turned, and within a second, he had disappeared in the darkness of the woods. Our attention was turned towards the old man. His clothes must have been rags from the beginning, because now they were little more than strips of cloth stuck to his body with blood and sweat. Mrs. Tibbins shone her light on his face, and we could see that he was alive, but panting as if his breathing was considerably impaired. As the light of the lantern examined his body, a great wound drowned in a pool of blood on his abdomen became visible. He tried to cover it with his hands, but they were too small to do so. It was apparent that he had little more than minutes left on this earth, so I leaned down and looked him in the eyes.

"Who did this to you? Please help us catch this monster!"

I could see in his eyes that he had heard my plea, but his laboured breathing did not allow him to pause for speaking, and when he attempted it, all that came out of his mouth was blood.

"We cannot do much for him," said Mrs. Tibbins. "If we try and get him to the village, he will surely die on the way."

She had barely finished her sentence, before the old man surprised us by raising his upper body from the ground slightly, and with an effort that mobilised all his remaining strength, managed to utter something that sounded like:

"Poe!"

And when he had said this, with a horrible throaty whisper, he fell back on the ground and took his last breath. I grasped his wrist and felt his pulse stop.

"Dear God," Tibbins exclaimed.

I'm not sure if it was the man's death or the sight of his abdominal wound that caused him to cry out, for when I looked at it more closely, I could see his intestines protruding. It is always disheartening and grieving to be present at a man's moment of death, but in this case, the loss of life was not on my mind as much as the circumstances of the situation. How were we to remove the body from this place? What had happened to him? What was it Holmes had run after? Where, exactly, had Holmes run off to?

There was little point in running after Holmes. What we could do was carry the old man's body to our horses and strap it onto Holmes' vacant animal in order to transport it back to the village. I was reluctant to abandon Holmes so far from civilisation, however, and volunteered to remain while the Tibbinses rode off with the body. When they had left, I decided to survey the surroundings on horseback. This meant that I could not search the thick woods, but I had the advantage of being able to scan a much larger area than if I had gone on foot. I set off in the direction Holmes has gone, following the border of the forest, and after a while the trees became more scattered, and I came to a point where I surmised that Holmes' path would have led if he had continued in the same direction. I jumped off my horse and examined the ground, desperately trying to inspect it the way Holmes would have, but too excited to be able to infer anything conclusive. I remounted and, having no other alternative, continued in the same direction. I rode a good many miles, but at some point I must have lost my sense of direction, for eventually I found myself on the road that led into the village and before I knew it, I was in the village square, not far from the inn.

I was quite perplexed by this turn of events; it was almost as if the landscape had changed and the village had been relocated to the path I was following instead of its actual location. Or was I upset by what had happened so that I confused myself? I stood bewildered in the village square for a good while before I forced myself to accept that there was not much more I could do without first resting and gathering new strength. And so it was that I went to an uneasy bed that night, dissatisfied with how the evening had turned out and most unsure of whether I had done what I could for my vanished friend.

VI. The Secrets of an Old Shepherd

The following day brandished white clouds and a light breeze that pressed on the windowpanes as if it sought to compress the building. Soon after waking, I found that Tibbins had alerted all the relevant authorities regarding the death of the wild man, and since their representatives were all in the village already in preparation for the inquest of Rover Dalton, that was quickly done. This was indeed the day of the inquest, but if Holmes, who had not reappeared since the previous night, was to miss it, it might as well be the end of the whole adventure.

The proceedings were to take place in the village hall, where the largest room had been prepared for it. For the benefit of the audience, it was furnished with twenty-odd chairs of different shapes and sizes, as well as a few large tables with chairs for the main actors in the drama. Whoever had made these preparations, however, turned out to have greatly underestimated the general interest in this event, as when I came into the room all the chairs were already occupied and a massive crowd of local men and women were crammed into the vacant space between the furniture and the walls. I was forced to go to the inquest by myself, as I had neither seen nor heard from Holmes all morning. It was disheartening trying to find a spot in the auditorium from where I would have a satisfying view of the proceedings, and when I finally forced myself to settle for what I concluded to be the least inferior place in the room, I found myself trapped in a crowd of burly and loud-mouthed shepherds who were exchanging cigarrettes among themselves and chatted idly as if they were standing in the street.

On the chairs that had been placed at the very front of the auditorium, I could see the diminutive figure of Mr Brody, whom we had spoken to in the tavern, along with other local farmers, Superintendent Ferrett and a couple of police constables. Hardly had I taken my place before the inquest was underway. The presiding coroner was a man called Charles Fortescue, one of the men who had been present at Dalton's autopsy. The first person to be heard was Dr Stanley Collins, who described his impressions of the body and what he had found during his post mortem. He concluded that Dalton had died from a severe blow to the head, inflicted by some form of animal. The scratches on his chest were not fatal and had been delivered after his death.

"And then there is the matter of what was found in the dead man's abdomen…" Collins continued.

I, of course, knew what was to come, but neither the magistrate nor the audience did, and when Collins explained what he had found, the reaction of the people was one of horror, but there was also an undertone of recognition in the murmur that ensued. It seemed the legend that Tibbins had told us of was well known to them. The magistrate called for order and asked Dr Collins how he would account for the contents of the dead man's stomach.

"I have no explanation," he said. "However, since the autopsy I have heard of a local legend telling of a similar incident as the result of witchcraft. I can only report what I saw, and I asked a colleague to inspect the rabbits as well."

"Is this colleague present?" asked the magistrate.

"Yes, he is over there. Dr John Watson."

All heads turned towards me and I nodded in agreement with Collins' statement. The doctor was dismissed and the witness stand was now taken in turn by all the shepherds who had been present at the discovery of the body. Not much was new to me in the information that came from these interrogations. Two of the shepherds on their way home together had come across Dalton's body and their shouts had attracted yet another shepherd. It seemed that Dalton was lying just where many of the shepherds used to walk on their way home to the village. Some of them claimed to have heard the howl just a few minutes before, but no one had seen anything or anyone.

Next on the stand was Dalton's wife, a lanky, sad, but not unattractive woman by the name of Elizabeth. She approached the front bench slowly, showing slight signs of fear.

"Mrs. Dalton," began the coroner, "you were among the last persons to see Mr Dalton alive. When was this?"

"It was just before he went out after his supper to bring in the flock that was his responsibility."

"I see. And who looked after this flock when he was having his supper?"

"His flock was together with Robinson's flock, and he was on his way to him when this happened."

The coroner looked at Robinson, one of the shepherds previously questioned.

"I see," said he. "And did your husband appear troubled or anxious at supper?"

"Not more than usual."

"You mean to say he was often troubled?"

"Oh yes. He'd been that way ever since he came back from India."

"I see. He was a campaigner?"

"No, sir. He didn't fight in any battles, sir."

"Then he witnessed something else that traumatised him?"

"I don't know, sir. He never spoke to me about it. Of course, when those sheep were killed last week, he seemed more worried and said something about it at dinner."

"What did he say?"

"He said 'They can't keep it secret for much longer.' When I asked him what he meant, he just snorted and kept quiet. He wasn't much of a talker, sir."

The coroner didn't seem to think any further questions were necessary, as the purpose of the proceedings – establishing the time and cause of death – had been fulfilled, or at least they had come as close to the answers as they could hope to. Mrs. Dalton was dismissed, and the coroner retired, but the verdict was already apparent to everybody present: Rover Dalton was murdered by person or persons unknown. As I stood there in the crowd, I contemplated upon that one uncertain word in this sentence: person.

I was interrupted in my meditation by one of the shepherds standing next to me.

"Wot's gonna 'appen now, then?" he said, leaning towards me.

I couldn't avoid turning up my nose at the hideous stench emanating from him. His hair, covered by a wrinkled canvas hat, was in complete disarray and had the appearance of straw. He smelled of cow dung, and I noticed that his right cheek, which could just be glimpsed under the hair, was spattered with mud.

"We're waiting for the verdict, of course," I said quickly.

"All right, Watson, no need to be rude!"

The voice was now completely different, and one that I instantly recognised. For the first time, the old shepherd turned directly towards me, which allowed me to look beyond the superficial signs of dirt and decrepitude. Herein lay Holmes' genius when it came to disguises, not that he could mask himself beyond recognition, but that he would, by quite simple means, alter a few vital things in his appearance, thereby making him virtually unrecognisable even to a close friend. This time he hadn't even done anything to cover his face. He had just put on a dirty coat, a shabby straw hat, dishevelled his hair and smeared his cheeks with a bit of mud, but the appearance was so stereotypical that it dissuaded people from taking a second look. The shepherd staff that I had thought he was leaning on I now saw was just a tree branch, haphazardly broken off from a tree.

"Just keep pretending I'm a dirty old shepherd," he said, and I could hear by his tone of voice that this was a delicate situation. "I've been through quite a bit since I last saw you, old friend. I think we are ready to start the last act of this drama. If you are up to it, I do hope you will assist me in this."

"You can count on me, Holmes."

"There will be danger."

"Good. That means it's worthwhile."

"Well spoken, dear chap. Now, here's what we'll do. You go to the inn and get your service revolver, making sure you don't show it to anyone. Then you meet me round the back of this building. All clear?"

"Perfectly. Good to see you again, by the way."

"Likewise, Boswell."

I was quickly in and out of my room fetching my revolver, and hid it by sticking it in behind my braces. When I rounded the large brick edifice of the village hall, Holmes was standing there as promised. Upon seeing me, he immediately straightened his back and threw away the gnarled stick he had been leaning on into some nearby bushes.

"Quickly!" he said. "We must act while the trail is still fresh."

He started to walk briskly towards the east, where the village bordered on thick woodlands.

"Will you tell me what has happened to you, and what trail it is we are following?" I pleaded as I followed him.

"Of course! Please forgive my inconsideration, Watson, but I have been absorbed in the task of tracking our mysterious monster all night. And you know how single-minded I can become once I am hot on the scent."

"Yes, yes, apology accepted and all that. But what happened to you?"

"Well, I ran in the direction in which the murderer had disappeared, and after a while I could see him in front of me, if only a distant glimpse. But he had the speed of a racehorse and it was impossible to keep up with him. I must have run for at least a mile, stopping now and then to make sure I was going in the direction of his traces."

"But I followed you! And I saw nothing, either of you or the murderer."

"Oh, Watson! Your nobility knows no ends. But those woods are larger and more disorientating than you might think. However, as I came to a small clearing, the traces of the culprit simply stopped. It was as if the earth had just swallowed him up! And just as that expression came to me, I knew what the only solution must be. So I started inspecting that clearing, and quite soon I found, camouflaged by shrubs of blackberry, a stone hut, little more than a low wooden door and four walls made of large and jagged blocks of stone. It looked as if it had been standing there for centuries, and maybe it has. To my surprise, I found the door unlocked, and so I went in. Behind the door was a flight of stone steps, leading down into utter darkness. I almost gave up the idea of going down when I found lying by the foot of the door a pile of candle stumps and a matchbox. Lighting one of the longer stumps, I groped my way down the rough steps until I came to the bottom. Here, a long corridor started, its walls, floor and ceiling made of earth and blocks of stone. I walked a few yards, but could not see an end to the passage, nor could I hear any sounds to indicate that it was leading anywhere. I had to consider my options, and I concluded that, although I was reluctant to abandon such a clear trail, whatever I encountered at the end of this corridor, I would be quite helpless on my own, and decided that my chances were better above ground. Said and done, I retraced my footsteps back to the entrance, and continued my pursuit through the forest, in the same direction that the underground tunnel was leading. It did not take me many minutes before I could guess where the tunnel was leading. Far away through the trees, by the pale light of the moon, I could discern the grey façade of an Elizabethan manor house."

The revelation put me to a halt.

"Upper Slaughter Manor House!" I proclaimed.

"Quite so," said Holmes. "Very soon, I came up to the big house, and it could only have been there that the tunnel was leading. I watched the building from the safety of the trees, trying to decide what to do next, when I heard the sound of distant voices. I could see a few figures emerging from a door in a stable building behind the main house. They stood there talking for a few moments, and then one of them went into the house and the two others climbed into the driver's seat of a closed carriage and drove away. They were going in my direction, and I realised that I was hiding just where the woods gave way to a country road. I gathered that I had to act fast, and as the carriage hurtled past me, I ran out into the road, grabbed hold of the rear of the vehicle and managed to pull myself up into a seating position. We drove for the better part of an hour, leaving the woods behind us and going uphill and downhill, through several valleys. As we reached the end of our journey, I recognised the surroundings. We had come to Reginald Parker's farm. In order not to risk being seen by his men, I jumped off the carriage before it had passed the gates. From a hiding place in the adjacent bushes, I could see the carriage going up the drive and stopping in front of the dwelling house. From within it stepped a man whose silhouette I instantly recognised as that of Parker himself."

"Good God! What does all this mean, Holmes? Are both Parker and the lord of the manor somehow involved in this affair?"

"What we have are links that do not yet form a complete chain. Parker and people who work at the manor house are involved, yes, but in what? And what was it that killed the wild man? We need to come to the bottom of this once and for all!"

"But what did you do when you had arrived at Parker's farm?"

"By this time I was much too curious not to attempt anything at least slightly risky, so I moved closer to the house and tried to look in through the windows. I could see Parker in there with a few other men, but I hadn't been watching for more than a minute, when I felt a hand on my shoulder. I turned round and saw two large men sneering at me like a couple of mischievous goblins. They pushed me forward, and would probably have brought me to their employer, Reginald Parker, had I not made use of my knowledge of baritsu and overpowered them. I hurried from the scene and took shelter in a shed, which is where I found this hat and coat. Making as good a disguise as I could, I managed to come away from the farm before the news of my presence spread, and started the long walk back to the village. I arrived just in time for the inquest."

"My dear friend! You must be exhausted."

"Quite the contrary. I am determined to add the last bits to this puzzle before the end of this day."

We had been walking along a gravel road leading from the cluster of small houses in the outskirts of the village through woods that grew increasingly thick as we moved along. Now, the narrow road turned into a tree-lined avenue, and at the end of it was Upper Slaughter Manor. Framed by the green of the trees and the front lawns, its distinctive Cotswolds stone frontage loomed silently before us like an old scaly toad lurking in the grass. From the main building, a series of tall chimneys arose, and the avenue led up to an ornate entrance with the forbidding appearance of a fortress. By the gates, Holmes removed his shabby coat and hat and left them by the roadside, and combed back his hair with his hands as we carried on up the path.

"No use hiding one's identity anymore," he said.

VII. A Tale of Slaughter

"What is your plan?" I wondered as we were approaching the manor house. "What are you going to say to him?"

"I just want to have a chat. Talk a bit of local history."

"But we assume he is involved in the murders somehow, don't we?"

"We cannot be sure. If my experience of country squires is anything to go by, they generally have very little knowledge of what goes on in their stables. What I will do, though, is return this to him." He took out the old rusty fork that he had found next to Dalton's body.

"How do you know it's his?"

"His family crest is engraved on the hilt."

We came up to the front door and I pulled the bell handle. Seconds later the door was opened slightly and I could glimpse the face and shirtfront of a liveried servant.

"Good morning," said Holmes. "Is the squire in?"

The servant turned his head so that only one of his eyes was visible in the light that shone in.

"What's it to you?"

"We should like to speak to him. You might say it is rather pressing."

"Who is it, Bellamy?"

The voice came from deep within the house, and it made the butler turn, thereby opening the door a bit more. We looked over his shoulder, but the interior was pitch black, and we could see nothing. The butler looked at us again, eyed us for a moment, and then he stepped away from the door, wordlessly letting us inside.

We stepped into a magnificent hallway, decorated with coats of arms, old tattered banners and the odd ancestral portrait. There were hardly any sources of light, apart from the daylight that shone in through gaps in curtains and whatnot, which made it impossible to see the ceiling. At the farther end of the room was a staircase, and the top end of that was also shrouded in darkness. Halfway down it, stood a man wrapped in a dull dressing-gown.

"How do you do, gentlemen?" he said in a faint voice that still echoed across the enormous space.

"How do you do, Your Lordship?" said Holmes. Then he held up the fork. "Is this yours?"

I couldn't help but frown at his lack of tact. His Lordship only turned and started going up the stairs.

"Come this way, if you please."

We ascended the staircase solemnly, since that was the state of mind struck by our host. On the wall beside us hung portraits of the previous lords, and the sight of them made me contemplate the legacy resting on the shoulders of the present squire. Holmes made note of the pictures too, and he remarked upon the striking family resemblance.

"The Slaughters all seem to present a prominent jaw."

The squire, who was waiting for us in a small sitting room at the top of the stairs, had heard Holmes' words.

"That's one of the things people tend to emphasise when they want to substantiate the werewolf theory," he said.

The little room was as dark as the rest of the house. The windows were shuttered and curtains drawn. His Lordship sat in an armchair on the middle of a large brown rug, and next to him were two more chairs. Had they been placed there in anticipation of our visit? Whatever the case, we sat down in them. His Lordship continued:

"The oldest traces of the werewolf story go back to the sixteenth century. That was before the witchcraft craze. The lord of the manor at that time, Edward, was interested in magic and sorcery, as was indeed many nobles at that time, including some royalties. This was the age of John Dee and Edward Kelley. But this must have been picked up by the villagers, for very soon the local vicar writes in the parish accounts that several locals have claimed the squire is meddling with witchcraft. These rumours eventually turn into a story of Edward allowing himself to be enchanted. This enchantment makes it possible for him to turn into a wolf at will, and wolf attacks on the local sheep flocks, which did still occur at that time, are henceforth explained in that way. It is a simple case of the distance between nobleman and commoners turning into suspicion and hostility, but with a curious local twist. The legend has been brought up now and then since that time, further deepening the cultural chasm between the lords of the manor and the local farming community. As I grew up, I became gradually aware of its persistence through the intermittent contacts I had with the people in the village, and when it became the death of my father, I realised I had to flee from here."

"The death of your father?" I asked.

"It was the reason for his depression and subsequent suicide. He flung himself from the highest window in the house. That was when I joined the army and was sent to India as an officer."

"To India?"

"Yes. I was there for fifteen years. It is a horrible place, but I stayed there simply to keep away from my home. I travelled across the country, went to the Himalayas, to Afghanistan and Indonesia. It was in Indonesia that I met Parker."

"Parker?" I said. "Reginald Parker?"

"Oh yes. The most awful man I have ever had dealings with. At that time, he was going around Southeast Asia, buying and selling rare animals. He would often acquire them illegally from poachers, and he had a vast network of contacts with zoologists looking for animals for European zoos. He was completely unscrupulous, doing business only for the money and for the pleasure he found in trying to obtain the rarest of species. Now, for some reason he had struck a deal with a high-ranking British officer to sell a large mammal to him. He would keep it in his small private menagerie in Devon. This man had very powerful friends and he could do pretty much whatever he wanted to, and so he assigned me to escort the animal back to England. By then, I was quite tired of Asia, and I was looking for a way to go back home, so even though the whole affair seemed very dubious to me, I agreed to do it. The buyer also insisted that Parker went with us, and he seemed to want to go home to England just like me, so we became travelling companions. With me on the journey was also a young private assigned to the mission. His name was Dalton."

I glanced at Holmes, in whose face I had learned to read the rare signs of astonishment. I looked back at His Lordship.

"*That* Dalton?" I queried.

His Lordship nodded.

"That journey was to become the worst experience of my life, for there was something wrong with the beast in the cargo hold. Our ship was called Ceres, and it left Bombay with a crew of sixty men. On our way to the Suez canal, all went smoothly. This I later learned was because Parker had brought with him sedatives for the animal that calmed it, but he only had a limited supply, and the first days of the voyage he had been wasteful with them, and so they soon ran out. The first sign that something was wrong was when Parker approached me and said he needed Dalton with him to guard the animal. Dalton was a brave and fearless soldier, and he had no qualms against such an assignment, but the experience broke him down entirely. You see, this specimen was no ordinary representative of its species. It was clear that since its capture in the jungles of Borneo, it had been savagely beaten and treated so as to make it fierce and aggressive. It had been gradually transformed into the wildest and most brutal living thing I have ever laid eyes on. And as the power of the sedatives had worn away, its true nature emerged.

"Dalton spent the nights alone in the cargo room next to the cage. After only a few watches, he came to me, his eyes red from lack of sleep. It was clear that he wanted to convey his fear to me, but his sense of duty and his soldierly pride made it difficult for him. He said that the animal was stronger than he had expected, and that he feared it would soon break free from its cage. He asked not to be left alone with it again. Meanwhile, Parker neglected his duty to care for the animal, and dismissed Dalton's apprehensions as mere cowardice. But Dalton was no coward. And when the animal one night finally managed to break open the door of its cage, he fought it single-handed, facing a hell that I would not wish on any man. I can only imagine what it must have been like for him! The animal was almost twice his size, and had the strength of three full-grown men. When we came down into the cargo room the next morning, we found him unconscious next to the cage, his body covered in horrible wounds, his uniform torn to shreds. The creature was nowhere to be found.

"We searched the ship from top to bottom, but it must have found secret places to hide where no man would think of going. In retrospect, I think it must have made use of the ship's ventilation system, though I cannot think how it could have fitted through the portholes. Parker claimed that it had jumped overboard, and almost persuaded us to become relieved. Soon enough, however, he was proved wrong. One of the seamen were found one morning on deck, literally torn asunder. And in the following days, the number of corpses increased, so that eventually there were about three or four casualties a day. Meanwhile, we were in the middle of the Mediterranean, several days from the nearest port. Our captain wanted to head for the coast of Italy, but Parker was adamant that we stayed on our charted course, referring to our employer, who would not be lenient in his punishment if we failed to reach our goal. And after that, the deaths suddenly stopped, so that we had reason to believe the animal had gone overboard. We were of course also afraid of what our employer might do should we fail, but naturally we all wondered if it really was worth it for the sake of a rare animal in a private zoo.

"We passed through the strait of Gibraltar without going ashore, afraid that the local officers would wish to come aboard and then find our inescapably illegal cargo. We had come a long way up the coast of Portugal, and were in the Bay of Biscay, when the creature struck again. It was as if it had been waiting for a final murdering rampage, for in one night alone, it ran berserk through the cabins, slashing to death twenty ship's mates with its hideous claws. The last days on board the Ceres turned into an ongoing hunting party. We caught sight of the animal several times, but it was extraordinarily fast and could disappear almost anywhere. A few times I swear I hit him with a pistol shot, but it was as if he could withstand such injuries. With only a day's journey left, we hit upon a plan of luring him back into his cage, which we had since repaired and strengthened. It was a dangerous plan, using ourselves as bait, but it was successful, and the animal was finally back in its cage after weeks of blood-soaked butchery. The Ceres reached the port of Southampton with a remaining crew of six people."

"My God," I whispered. "What a story! It is truly amazing that you escaped unscathed, Your Lordship."

"Well, almost," he replied, opened his dressing gown and pulling up his shirt. On his abdomen were three large scars, identical to the wounds on Rover Dalton and the old hermit.

"And what happened when you arrived in England?" asked Holmes.

"That was when a horrible episode turned into a perpetual curse. We managed, with the help of our military authority and the connections of our employer, to get the animal off the ship without the knowledge of the customs officers. But when we met the man who had purchased this beast, and when he saw how wild it was, and what it had done during the journey, then of course he didn't want anything to do with it. He ordered us to destroy it. I volunteered to do it, as it would have been quite a catharsis after what I had lived through, but then Parker insisted on taking care of it. I didn't object, though I should have been suspicious of this. My experience now made me feel quite homesick, and I was suddenly anxious to go home to Upper Slaughter. The journey had turned poor Dalton into a shadow of his former self, and to try and facilitate his return to England and his family, I offered him to move into a farm in Upper Slaughter. I thought the tranquillity of the Cotswolds would do him good. I couldn't have been more wrong.

"Within months of returning here, there was a knock on the front door, and Bellamy let in the visitor. It was Parker. He had gone into sheep farming and had just acquired a large farm nearby. But this did not mean he would refrain from his old ways. In fact, he came here with the expressive purpose of extortion. He wanted me to allow him to increase the proceeds from his farming without increasing my share. And he wanted free hands to buy land and to strike deals so that the farms under Upper Slaughter Manor, though still in name under me, were to all intents and purposes under his supervision. It was a mad and evil affair, and I rejected it outright. But he had a hold on me, he said, and he wanted me to come outside.

"He took me around the house to the stables at the back, which I hadn't made use of in years. There we found a congregation of large and dangerous-looking men who were evidently in Parker's employ. I was escorted inside, and was met with a devastating sight. There, in the stables, a large cage had been installed. And inside the cage was the monster that we had taken back from India. Parker had kept it, realising it would be useful to him. So, like a medieval rogue, threatening to throw his enemies to the dragon, he used it to wield power. He said that he would reveal my involvement in the Ceres affair if I did not cooperate. He said that he would lock me in with the animal. At the same time, while glad to be home after all my escapades, there was no love lost between myself and the locals, due to what happened to my father. I see now that I failed to fathom the full extent of Parker's plans, and how they would impact the local sheep farmers. I simply didn't care what befell the people here because of the grudge I bore. My resistance to Parker, perhaps, was too feeble. When I had given in to him, and he realised his plans, I slowly became aware of what I had done. His men, grim-looking chaps hired from the criminal classes, were soon hanging about the place, guarding the animal in the stables, or guarding me. But Parker's reasons for keeping the animal were not limited to threatening me. His plan was also to use it in aid of his plan to suppress the local farmers. For he had found out before coming here, that this was a very superstitious place, and that legends of a monster were still very much in the air among the simpler people. If he could produce such a monster, and imply that he had the power over it, then he would have power over the people and their sheep. So he would let the animal out on occasion, not without supervision, naturally, but he would chain it to a tree in the woods or place the cage in a hidden place where it would howl all night, scaring the people who dwelled nearby. His plan was very successful for a long time. But he hadn't counted on one thing: Dalton.

"Parker had no idea that Dalton had taken residence in Upper Slaughter. And Dalton didn't know of Parker's presence, until word about the new and prosperous sheep farmer got round. Dalton started to get suspicious, and then one night he came upon the animal in its cage where it was standing hidden in a grove of trees. He recognised his old adversary immediately and all the old wounds were reopened. He came to me, believing that I was responsible for bringing it here. I explained to him about Parker, and he swore that he would destroy both the animal and Parker. I wished him luck, and I presented him with the best weapon I could find in the house, an old sharp fork used of old to spear meat. It was larger and sharper than any of the knives in the household, and we haven't had ammunition for our hunting rifles for years. Dalton took it and gave word to Parker, arranging a meeting. Meanwhile, Parker was having problems with the animal. It broke loose from its watchers and killed a flock of sheep. And Dalton was too confused and emotional to think straight! It was obvious that Parker would bring his men and the animal to the meeting. I was not present at the scene, but I can picture it. Them letting it loose on poor Dalton, and then watching as it finished him off. Well, what was I to do? I haven't been out of this house for years! I wouldn't know the first thing to do. What can I do?"

"You could have gone to the police," I said.

"I was kept under watch, there was nothing I could do."

"What about the hermit?" asked Holmes.

"Hermit?" said His Lordship. "What hermit?"

Holmes explained about the attack on Hob.

"Good God!" cried His Lordship. "Not another one. They really have lost control of it. And I can imagine how they are treating it, beating and wounding it to aggravate it. Whenever it is released it goes mad! In connection to the stables there is an old secret passageway, leading from the stables out into the woods. In the middle of it is an old priest hole used in Elizabethan times to hide the local priests from persecution. I believe they used the passage to let the creature out. The hermit must have been residing in close proximity to the entrance."

His Lordship leaned forward and hid his face in his hands. He was a wreck of a man, dressed in worn-out clothes, his face unshaved and tired-looking. When I considered the tale he had just told us, I couldn't help but sympathise with the man and what he must have been through. I had no doubt, however, that he now was a mentally weak and apathetic man, who was indirectly an accomplice in this whole affair, if only through his passivity.

Holmes was looking at him sternly, not showing much sign that he was gratified at all the information he had been given.

"May we see it?" he said.

His Lordship looked up.

"See it?"

"The animal."

His Lordship closed his eyes.

"If you so wish."

"Yes, let me show it to you!" The voice had come from the staircase behind us. As we turned, we saw there on the landing, a smug-looking man in tweeds, flanked by two large brutes. The man in the middle was smiling broadly. "I am most anxious to show it to you, Mr Holmes," he continued. "It might be interesting to you as a man of science. I would even be prepared to let you go in the cage with it!"

His companions laughed. Holmes rose from his chair.

"Very good. Let us see it."

I felt that he was being foolish, but said nothing. When he started moving towards the stairs, I followed. I understood that the man in tweed was Reginald Parker, but I recognised him as the stout man who had been present at Dalton's post mortem. He looked at us as we started to walk down the stairs, and led us out of the house. We left His Lordship behind us, sitting trapped in his big armchair.

"It was no mystery where you had run off to, Mr Holmes," said Parker as we went. "I have eyes and ears all over this village."

"Yes," said Holmes, glancing at Parker's men. "And from the looks of it, not much brains behind the eyes and ears."

We came out of the house, went round the back and found the stables, where more men were waiting. Holmes, who was still in the front of our parade, stopped abruptly in front of one of the men, and looked at him. Then, without flinching, he pulled his cigarette from between his lips. The man was so surprised that he didn't even respond with anger. Holmes studied the cigarette.

"Slovenian, eh?"

The man took it back.

"From my home country," he said with a distinct accent. "Better than English."

Holmes looked him in the eyes.

"Hope you enjoyed the show," he said and moved on.

The other men looked baffled, but to Holmes and the Slovenian, it was clear that Holmes was referring to the murder of Dalton.

We came up to the door of the stable building. Here, Parker took the lead and let us in. I was quite unprepared for what I was about to see, and from His Lordship's tale I had no guesses as to the identity of the mysterious creature. Inside, one of the boxes had been converted into a large cage, its barred walls reaching up to the ceiling. From the entrance, we couldn't see what was inside it. It was clear that whatever lived in the cage was hiding in the corner. Moving closer to it, I could make out something furry, but we had barely had time to see before it jumped out of its hiding-place and threw itself at the bars, screaming loudly and beating its fists in the air. If the bars hadn't been there, we would all have been killed within seconds. The sight of the animal was unspeakable, and yet I could not take my eyes off it. It wasn't very tall, but the mass of its body was still the size of two men put together. It was covered in red and grey fur, and it had scars all over its body.

"What is it?" was all I could muster.

"It's an orangutan!" replied Holmes. "An Indonesian man-ape. But an unusually large specimen, and one that has been considerably undomesticated with the way it has been treated by humans."

To hear Holmes explain it like this in his calm voice was reassuring, and I almost started to feel a bit sorry for this pathetic creature, and maybe even understand its grudge against humanity.

"There's your werewolf, gentlemen," said Parker. "Much more vicious and lethal than anything than can be conjured up by imagination. I hate to put a premature end to our acquaintance, Mr Holmes. I quite enjoyed your little visit the other day, but I may have pretended to know less about you than I do, and I really cannot allow you two to get in the way of my plans. Roberts! Unlock the cage door!"

One of Parker's men stepped forward with a big batch of rusty keys, while another pushed us towards the cage. At the same moment, Holmes leaned slightly towards me and whispered:

"Watson! Ayo gorkhali!"

I was baffled by this strange utterance, but a second later I identified the war cry of the Gurkha Rifles, and realised that Holmes was using it to instigate a manoeuvre that would be unintelligible to the others. I had only one way of heeding the call, and as we came to the door of the cage, I swiftly pulled out my revolver. At the same time, Holmes grabbed the arm of the man behind us and, with the assistance of his martial arts skills, threw him against the man with the keys, making them both fall over in a large pile next to the cage. It was now apparent to me that this gesture was minutely timed, for the cage had just been unlocked, and in the next moment, Holmes took hold of Parker, who was given no time to react, and threw him into the cage. Parker screamed madly, and the rest of his henchmen took a step forward, but I managed to keep them at bay with the help of my weapon.

Parker started to shake the cage door while his pet approached behind his back. Holmes only produced the rusty old fork found with Dalton's body and handed it to him.

"Use this," he said. "I will give you the same chance that Dalton had."

The thickset henchmen came nearer, and the guns they produced dwarfed my simple service revolver. Holmes and I stepped aside and moved towards the exit. I cocked my pistol in order to make my threats seem convincing, and when we were a few steps from the door, we hurried out, knowing that the men would first rush forward to rescue Parker before coming after us. From what I saw just before we ran out of the stables, Parker would be let out of the cage just seconds before his orangutan slashed him with its sharp claws.

VIII. Wolf's Bane

Coming out of the stables, we had no option but to run as fast as we could away from the manor house. We knew, of course, that Parker and his men were not far behind, as they would pursue us the moment they had managed to get Parker out of the cage. Holmes insisted that we went through the woods instead of using the road to make it more difficult for our pursuers. My old leg wound was not completely happy with this decision, but I had to try and forget the pain unless I wanted to be caught and dragged back to the monster. After a few minutes, I was heartily relieved to glimpse the houses of the village between the trees. Holmes knew exactly what to do. He led the way straight to the village hall, and found the relevant authority figures still lingering there after the inquest. Superintendent Ferrett of the Gloucestershire Constabulary accosted Holmes and they spoke for a few minutes while I waited to one side with my revolver in my trouser pocket. I couldn't quite hear what was said, but suddenly Ferrett called for his men, loudly ordering one of them to fetch more officers. Then he raised his voice before the crowd of shepherds and other spectators still hanging about.

"Gentlemen! We have an emergency. We need your help. In a few minutes Dalton's murderer will show up in the village square together with his accomplices. Will you help us arresting them?"

The men looked at each other, some frowning, others mumbling sceptically.

"Who is it?" said a voice at the back.

"The man's name is Reginald Parker!" said Holmes.

Upon hearing this name, all of them stepped forward to enlist in the manhunt. Cries of "At last" and "Go get your pitchforks, lads" could be heard in the ensuing enthusiasm. Ferrett implored them to proceed in an orderly fashion and ushered them out into the square. Here we were met with Parker and his men, and the sight of them caused the crowd to run towards them. Parker gesticulated feverishly, trying to invoke his authority as employer.

"Please, gentlemen! There has been a gross misunderstanding."

But the men, egged on by years of repressed frustrations finally brought to a boil, moved closer, and Parker's henchmen slowly realised that they were completely outnumbered. Suddenly, someone in the crowd let out a wolf's howl, like the one that was heard in church during Tibbins' service. Some of the men replied with laughter, others by echoing the howl, and within seconds, the entire mass of shepherds was howling like mad, creating an atmosphere so menacing that Parker's men simply threw down their weapons while Parker himself stood in the middle, looking helpless and panic-stricken.

Ferrett, Holmes and myself worked together to make the following proceedings as civilised as possible, but it was difficult to prevent the sensation of the lynch mob emerging, and at one critical moment, I almost feared that Parker would be burned at the stake. Although Parker may have suffered a few blows, the worst scenario was avoided and the culprits were eventually locked up in the cellar of the village hall.

I shan't go into too much detail about the subsequent detention of Parker and his men or the capture of the orangutan, except to say that Parker's guilt was apparent and that the animal was examined by zoo keepers but was deemed too mentally traumatized by its experiences and had to be put down. His Lordship was charged with assisting Parker and withholding information, but was eventually acquitted in court, and he returned to an increasingly harmonious existence in his manor house. The dissolution of Parker's land was a welcome transformation for the local farmers, although this was a time of significant changes in the agricultural landscape of England, and the national implementation of enclosure, that had been neglected by Upper Slaughter when Parker had brought bigger problems, made it impossible for the small-scale farmers of this area to go back to their old ways. Within a few years, wealthy farmers not unlike Parker, but within the bounds of the law, had turned this region into a prosperous industrial-scale farmland, unfit for the smallholder.

When the business surrounding the arrest of Parker and the spreading of the solution to the murders had alleviated a few days later, Holmes and I were invited to the vicarage for one final dinner before it was time for us to leave. All evening, we scrutinised and dissected every little detail of what had happened, and Mr and Mrs. Tibbins had quite a few questions to put to Holmes about how one thing was connected to the other. Towards the end of the evening, as we enjoyed a delicious trifle prepared by the cook, Mrs. Tibbins exclaimed in conclusion to it all:

"What a perfectly unlikely turn of events! That our little village should be the final dwelling place of two soldiers from India, a dealer in rare animals and a ferocious baboon…"

"Orangutan, my dear," corrected the vicar.

"A ferocious *orangutan*," amended his wife.

"Which of course explains the presence of handprints on the scene of Dalton's murder," remarked Holmes. "The feet of an orangutan are curiously similar to human hands, although of a slightly different appearance."

"It also explains old Hob's last word," said Tibbins. "'Poe.' Hob was a wild man, but he was also quite well-read, and had once worked as a schoolmaster. When he lay dying he was anxious to indicate to us that he had been attacked by the same animal that Edgar Allan Poe used as a culprit in one of his stories."

Mrs. Tibbins giggled.

"But it is all so utterly improbable!"

"I cannot agree with you, Mrs. Tibbins," I replied. "When you consider that this country stretches across the globe, incorporating all sorts of people in all walks of life imaginable, it isn't all that uncanny."

"Well, Dr Watson, of course you're a man of the world!" retorted Mrs. Tibbins acerbically. "What do I know?"

"But the most interesting features of this case," said Holmes, "are the ones that are indigenous to this village. The community of shepherds and their ways of life, the hard work of the vicar in his attempts to congregate the locals in his church, the way this strange landscape affects the minds and fantasy of the people in it. And most intriguing of all, I find, is the local folklore and the different ways the people here relate to it. There are the peasants and their oral and primitive traditions handed down through generations, quite unchanged for centuries. Then there are the wealthier people of this village and their rather more lightweight approach to it, seeing it as curiosities to be collected like butterflies and displayed on the walls. And then we have you, vicar, who are somewhere in between, not sharing the beliefs of the locals and looking at them with bewildered amusement, while at the same time forced to take them seriously as you fight paganism in the name of Christianity. And your fascinating art collection in the adjacent room certainly hints at an even more complex attitude than that. Maybe your time here has turned you into a mixture of pagan and Christian, much like those first converts of these islands, who were quite reluctant to abandon their old ways?"

The vicar smiled impenetrably at Holmes.

"I have just read a most thought-provoking new book," continued Holmes. "'The Golden Bough' by James Frazer, a Scottish anthropologist, who presents the thesis that human belief develops through three stages. From the belief in magic we evolve to religion, and from religion we evolve to science. I am a man of science, myself, and I should very much like to think that Dr Frazer is correct, but what I have seen here makes me wonder. Is not our modern science a new, albeit improved, version of the science that Archimedes or Copernicus worked in? And is the belief in magic dead due to the emergence of religion and science? Not so. All three of them coexist in all times, that would be my thesis. However, Parker took advantage of a piece of local folklore in his extortionist ways, which makes me think that there is danger in the foolish and primitive beliefs of superstitious peasants."

Tibbins leaned forward, eager to counter with thoughts of his own.

"Your observations are most ingenious, Mr Holmes. I have read Mr Frazer's book too, and find it most exhilarating. But I have encountered so much superstition in my work, and I start to believe, not in the magic itself, but in its seductive powers. In this village, and elsewhere, not even people of education, who have lived apart from the traditions of simpler folk, can withstand magic and folklore."

"I must confess," I said, "that Parker almost had me believing in magic when he staged that little scene with the baby rabbits. It was so convincing, and I only fell for it because I did not recognise Parker. I supposed that is why they only called for me. Holmes would have suspected something."

"It was an extravagant and slightly too bold attempt at deterring us," said Holmes. "Its credibility rested to some extent on its utter strangeness, but Parker again relied on his knowledge of the local folklore. This time, though, I think he underestimated the people he tried to deceive."

"Perhaps he took you for gullible amateur enthusiasts, like myself or Colonel Draycot," said Tibbins.

"Now you are underestimating yourself, vicar," replied Holmes amiably.

"Well, as I said, I know from experience the seductive powers of folklore on gentleman amateurs. They pursue it as if it had some secret knowledge within, or as if there was a final solution to riddles of the supernatural. I recognised that pursuit in myself as well. But magic is all about riddles without solutions, questions without answers, and learning that some problems can never be solved. And that is a wisdom that both religion and science are lacking!"

Holmes smiled gently.

"I have often failed in my profession, vicar," he said. "But it was not because there was no solution to the problem, but because I was too obtuse. And when religion and science fail, it is not because humans are too persistent in trying to find an answer when there isn't one, but because they are stupid."

We all laughed, and Mrs. Tibbins raised her glass.

"In that case, I propose a toast to stupidity!"

Holmes looked at her as if to contradict her, but seemed to change his mind, and raised his own glass too.

The Adventure of the Velvet Lampshade

As I leaf through my rather scant notes on the cases that I experienced in the very beginning of my long association with Sherlock Holmes, I often struggle to recall the details. I find mention of the mystery of the one-eyed nursemaid, the affair of the schoolboy conspiracy and the series of seemingly unrelated riddles that brought us face to face with the Monster of Gravesend, most occurrences of which I have only vague recollections. But among these there is one matter that stands out from the rest, if only because of the trifling quirk that was at the centre of it. It began on an uneventful afternoon in mid-January, that time of the year when all the commotion of Christmas leaves after it a gaping hole, and occasional gales remind one of the immense distance of spring.

Holmes and I were sitting by the fire, he enveloped in a thick cloud of pipe smoke, and I engrossed in a collection of Lamb's essays, while a mixture of rain and snow slowly covered the windows. Not a word had been spoken between us for nearly half an hour, when suddenly Holmes raised his hand to remove his pipe from his mouth.

"Is it serious?" he asked, quite sincerely.

"Serious?" I said, without raising my eyes from my book.

"Simkins' illness."

This remark, however, could not keep me from looking up at him.

"Simkins?"

"The waiter at your club. I understand that he was absent at lunch today."

"Who told you?"

"You did."

"I did nothing of the sort!"

"Quite involuntarily, but all the same. You see, Simkins is a very professional and meticulous man, and judging from the customary state of your carnation, I would surmise that he always makes sure he removes it when he is brushing your coat, putting it back when he is finished. But today, your buttonhole is in a deplorable state, and I can only conclude that it is the cavalier brushwork of his replacement that is the culprit, for your overcoat would only flatten it, not rip its petals in this way. And since I know you are always served by Simkins, I gather he was indisposed."

I looked down at the pale little flower in my buttonhole and smiled. Then I looked back up at Holmes.

"Pneumonia, they say, but he's recovering."

"Glad to hear it," said Holmes with a smile.

I tried to return to the solemnity of my reading, but Holmes had distracted me irrevocably, and so I put it to one side.

"Is there something on your mind?" I queried.

"Save boredom, nothing. I fear that the weather is too intimidating for anyone to leave home, when quite possibly hundreds of Londoners sit around with remarkable conundrums that would take my mind off ennui."

"If their vexation is considerable enough, I'm sure they will seek your assistance."

"Yes, but that is truly it. Nobody does anything at this time of year, and so they don't get into trouble. And the few that do, get involved in such trifling matters that they see no point in braving the weather to find a solution."

"Not true!" I said, and picked up the morning's copy of *The Times* which lay in a muddle on the hearthrug. "Why, here on the front page is the news of a bank robbery in Islington! And then an update on the state visit from the sultan of Brunei."

"Well, maybe I'm overreacting," Holmes sighed. "You know how inertia plays tricks with my nerves."

"Perhaps an early bed would be the proper medicine?"

Holmes turned his head.

"No, that would be premature, for unless I'm mistaken that was the doorbell. In a few minutes we shall know whether it is a client whose problems are large enough for him to forget about the weather conditions."

We did find out, and to Holmes' great satisfaction, a woman soon enough stepped in through our door. She was a tall and healthy-looking lady, dressed in a long black coat spattered with sleet, and a broad hat, decorative but robust enough to withstand the current climate. The minute she entered, it was clear to me that she was a confident and forthright woman, of the kind that a man must have considerable confidence in himself to take as wife. Holmes stepped forward and greeted her, inviting her to take a seat by the fire.

"Thank you, Mr Holmes," she said in a severe and attractive voice. "My name is Mrs. Olivia Trubshawe, and I have come to you from Pangbourne, where I live with my husband."

"You left your home in a hurry, I see," remarked Holmes. "You have missed a button in your blouse and the gloves you so swiftly picked up as you went out do not match the rest of your clothes, if you forgive me for saying so."

The woman looked down at herself, quickly remedied her button and crossed her arms, as if to make us forget about it.

"I'm sorry for my appearance," she said. "The matter is a pressing one."

Holmes made a grand gesture.

"Please do not apologise for anything, Mrs. Trubshawe. The imperfections in your appearance were only apparent thanks to the absolute perfection in the rest of it. Lay your matter before me and my colleague, and we shall do what we can to make you choose your gloves with more care in the future."

"Well," she began, "as I said, we live at Pangbourne. Our house is a substantial one, which my husband inherited from his uncle, who built it but had no family of his own to leave it to. It's called Frogmore End and due to its size it requires rather a large number of staff. Since I married my husband George and moved into the house, I have been obliged to develop into a skilled head of the household, as George works in the City, and I would like to think that in these four years of marriage, I have turned into a competent supervisor of the domestic work. You see, I have quite strong opinions about servants and how they should be treated, and have made it my business to make sure that they have decent working conditions, and that I get acquainted with all whom we employ. I am a realistic woman, and I know that we could not occupy a house such as ours without employing our staff, and these people are always grateful for the work opportunity, but I have more radical views concerning those who live in smaller quarters but are still pampered with like little children.

"But this is by the way. I have come to you now because one of our chambermaids, a Miss Julia Burton, has gone missing. She has been with us for six months and has been a hard-working and polite servant. She is only nineteen, and with some girls of that age it is difficult to deter them from ill-advised romantic entanglements, with men both inside and outside the house, but Julia, though not a prim girl, has always approached her work with a professionalism quite unusual for her age. She is from London, but her only relation – her mother – died a few years ago. She previously worked at the London household of an old widow and when she died, she sought a place with us, having been recommended to do so by one of our previous employees. I have developed quite an eye for suitable young men and women, and so it didn't take me long to see that she was a decent sort of girl and that she would do nicely.

"It is now four days since she disappeared. There was nothing to suggest that anything would happen before that. The evening before, I saw her in the dining room as she was clearing the table and she smiled when she noticed me. Then the next morning, our housekeeper informed my husband and me that she had not come down to breakfast and when a footman had went up to her room, it had been empty. All her things were still there, however, and the bed had not been slept in. We initiated an informal questioning of the entire staff, but no one had heard or seen anything strange during the night. The house and the grounds have been searched without producing any clues. But then strange things started to happen. Some of the maids claimed to have seen a man in the grounds of the house, stealing among the oak trees around the driveway. They were quite upset, as he was apparently a burly sort of creature, all dressed in black. The reports were puzzling, no doubt, but my husband and I took little notice of them even though more people claimed to have seen this stranger. And then this morning, I saw him myself. I was on the terrace at the back of the house, and could quite clearly see the figure of a large man standing at the further edge of the pond looking straight at the house. I went to fetch George, but when we returned the man was gone. This incident alarmed me so much that I insisted upon going to London to call for your assistance."

The lady, who had been speaking very quickly, finally had time to catch her breath. Holmes was slumped very deep in his easy chair, and as the woman finished her narrative, he started to wave his hands about.

"Please, Mrs. Trubshawe, I wish you wouldn't protect your employee. It makes it quite impossible for me to help you if you're going to keep the truth from me."

Our visitor rose from her seat and so did I.

"Holmes!" I exclaimed. "That's no way to speak to a lady."

Mrs. Trubshawe looked as if she was going to say something in agreement with me, but seemed to have trouble finding the words. Instead Holmes, who was still sitting at ease, explained himself.

"Come, come, Mrs. Trubshawe. It is quite obvious why you have come to us and not the police. You know that if you consult them, they will discover Miss Burton's criminal record and be prejudiced against you."

"Holmes, you have no proof of your allegations!"

"Only this woman's presence in our room. And her — shall we say, generous attitude to her servants? Perhaps your efforts to run an efficient household have been replaced by the ambition to run a charity operation for reformed criminals who wish to make a decent living? Sit down, Mrs. Trubshawe, please. And you too, Watson, you're being much too chivalrous. There. Now, I am not judging you or your wish to help those who are worse off than you. I'm sure the shock of moving in to an enormous house, you coming from a humble background yourself as that slight ruggedness in your speech betrays, made you feel it was your duty. Well, why not? Our age needs initiatives like that. I will of course help you find your charge, but you must tell me all about her, or else my equation will miss a vital factor."

Mrs. Trubshawe sat down slowly on her chair like a schoolgirl who has just been caught in the middle of a prank.

"Very well, Mr Holmes. It is true as you say, Julia has a previous conviction. As, indeed, do many of the people we employ. But I refuse to believe that it has anything to do with the current state of affairs. She fell in with a bad sort of people when she was with her previous employer in London.

When you're in service in central London you congregate with the people who frequent the local haunts. And the people who fraternise in the mews and the public houses are not the same as the ones that occupy the terraced houses and who only know the street by walking from their front doors to their coaches. Julia met a man at the pub where the maids and the footmen used to go when off duty. He was very persuasive and domineering, and a young impressionable girl like Julia was no match for him. They became a couple, or at least he started to consider himself her suitor, and he started to pester the house where she worked, demanding to see her and often showing up drunk at the back door. One day he came to blows with one of the stable lads, and managed to break his nose, after which he was arrested. Julia was identified as an accomplice, and was also charged with assault. As a consequence of this, she was given her notice. The man had a few previous offences on his record and was sent to prison. Julia was fined."

"And I trust Miss Burton had trouble finding work after that?" said Holmes.

"Yes. The agency warned me when I wanted to hire her, but after meeting her I was sure I had made the right decision. What has happened these past few days is a great surprise to me. There is nothing, absolutely nothing, in Julia's conduct when she has been with us to suggest that something like this would happen. She has behaved impeccably throughout and has even shown signs of an aspiring artistic vein. When the rest of the household asks her to come along for a pot of beer, she turns them down and prefers to sit by herself in the house with her sketchbook in front of one of our old paintings."

Holmes had been sitting motionless in his chair since Mrs. Trubshawe began her narrative, looking quite bored and skeptical, as was his habit before assessing whether our visitor's problem was strange enough to interest him. As the gracious lady put a stop to her account, however, I could detect a couple of faint twitches in the corner of his mouth, which almost amounted to a smile. This was enough for me to conclude that Holmes' curiosity had been aroused.

"Mrs. Trubshawe," he began, "if your maid has been gone these four days, there is not much I can do. Whether she has been abducted or left by her own choice, she has a head start which is large enough for her to be out of the country or even this continent by now. What I can do, perhaps, is shed some light on the mystery. I might be able to make some observations on the nature of her disappearance or piece together her last few hours in the house. I cannot promise you more than that."

The woman looked Holmes sternly in the eyes like a patient receiving a troubling diagnosis from a physician.

"That would be more than welcome," she said. "If you wish, you can accompany me back to Pangbourne tonight. The house, as I said, is large and it would be easy for us to prepare two beds for you."

"Splendid! You wouldn't object to a small outing, would you, Watson? I trust the bedrooms at Frogmore End are much more comfortable than anything Baker Street may offer."

Within two hours of our leaving Baker Street, we were jolting up the bridleway of Frogmore End in the Trubshawes' private carriage. The ride from Pangbourne station had been quite a long one, but the sight of the large house with its rows of windows glowing with a warm light made my mind easier. The house was a heavy pile of gothic revival, arranged in a jumble of turrets and wings that made me think that the maze of corridors inside it must be a veritable nightmare for a servant with a tray. We were met on the front steps by Mr Trubshawe, a handsome man with a dashing moustache, but whose short stature was blatantly obvious when he was standing next to his wife. He greeted us with a beaming smile and appeared very civil, but somehow I received the impression that he was not as engaged in this whole business as his wife. Mrs. Trubshawe was a strong willed woman with an admirable social conscience, but Mr Trubshawe seemed to me the epitome of the modern businessman, assiduous, but ultimately dull and uncharismatic, and I speculated to myself on how their match had come about.

As we were shown through the house, my premonitions concerning its internal maze were confirmed. A very young-looking footman with a pale and serious face took care of our luggage while Holmes expressed his wish to see Miss Burton's private quarters. We were taken to a long and cramped corridor at the very top of the house with a row of minuscule servant bedrooms.

"It might look very simple at first sight," Mrs. Trubshawe remarked, as if to explain the heartless cruelty of letting the servants sleep in anything smaller than a ballroom, "but we see to it that everyone has their own room, you see, and so we have to make use of these rather old-fashioned little chambers."

Julia Burton's room was at the end of the corridor and to me it seemed like quite a comfortable and cosy place, with a small mullioned window overlooking the ridge of a roof. Her bed was neatly made, and on a table lay a small collection of hairbrushes and toiletries which wouldn't look out of place in any girl's bedroom. On the walls were some of her drawings, put up with tacks, and at a glance I could see some rather well made impressions of Rubens and Gainsborough. To my eyes, it really seemed as if Miss Burton had just stood up and walked out of the room. Holmes, though, would probably not be content with such a notion, and he paced the room looking around with piercing eyes. When an examination of the table and the windowsill left him dissatisfied, he went down on his knees to study the floor. I noticed it was exceedingly dusty.

"Yes, well," commented Mrs. Trubshawe. "The idea is that everyone is in charge of cleaning their own room, but of course they very seldom have the time to do so."

Holmes came to his feet, and motioned me to join him by the side of the bed.

"Watson. Would you help me to move the bed a bit?"

"How far?"

"Just to the other end of the room would suffice."

We grabbed hold of one end each, and shifted it so that the floor underneath it became fully exposed.

"Mr Trubshawe," said Holmes. "Will you please come here with that lamp?"

Trubshawe had been carrying a paraffin lamp during our tour of the house, and when he came across the room to where we were standing, it lit up the floor in the corner. We could now quite clearly see how a rectangle of floor, roughly the size of a dinner tray, was completely free from the dust that lay in such a thick layer over the rest of the floor.

"How peculiar," said Trubshawe. "What are we to make of that?"

"Nothing just yet," replied Holmes. "But we must commit it to memory."

Holmes and I repositioned the bed, and with that Holmes appeared to be satisfied.

"Is there anything else you wish to see?" asked Mrs. Trubshawe.

"Only our bedroom," said Holmes.

Mrs. Trubshawe seemed slightly confused by this answer, but did not complain, and so we were taken from the servants' quarters and back down into the main house. The way to our allotted chambers was a long one, however.

"We shall have to put you in the east wing," said Mrs. Trubshawe on the way. "It is a part of the house we rarely use these days."

"I'm afraid my uncle suffered from delusions of grandeur," added Mr Trubshawe. "He was a bit more successful than is healthy for a man and bought up the contents of old castles from diminishing noble families, and then he had this great edifice built to contain it all. Died from a heart attack six months after it was finished."

We had been walking through a long gallery which now opened up to a vast room filled with objects crammed into every corner without much thought to decoration or organisation. There were sofas and chairs, tabletops full of vulgar sculptures and gold-plated statues, endless Persian rugs, one or two tiger skins and walls covered in paintings of all sizes. Curiously, however, there was only one lamp to light up the room. It was standing on a table in a corner, and only allowed us to get an inkling of the jumble in the rest of the room.

Mrs. Trubshawe sighed as we entered.

"My God. I had managed to forget about this room. It really is a bit of a burden."

"I pity the person who has to dust it all," I said.

"I don't think Uncle Alfred had much consideration for persons like that," said Mr Trubshawe.

"Your bedrooms are at the far end of this room," explained his wife, and we continued across the floor.

We had come to the table with the lamp, when Holmes stopped suddenly. He stood there for a while, inspecting the lamp. It was quite a substantial thing, with an ornate base and over the glass globe was a lampshade in thick dark-red velvet.

"Is anything the matter, Mr Holmes?" asked Mr Trubshawe.

Holmes stood there a moment longer, then turned to the rest of us.

"Hm? No, nothing. Let's push on."

We were shown to our bedrooms, which were located down a short corridor a few metres from the large room. The Trubshawes left us alone to get settled in, and informed us that dinner would be served shortly. I started to unpack my overnight bag as soon as I was left alone, but after only a couple of minutes Holmes re-entered, dressed for dinner.

"So," I said, "what do you make of it, old boy?"

Holmes sat on a wicker chair in the corner and produced a cigarette.

"It is quite plain to me, but a few more inquiries are necessary before I dare to speak. What I find infinitely more interesting, and what I think made me want to come here, is the Trubshawes' marriage."

I chuckled.

"The sight of the husband actually surprised me a bit. Why would such a characteristic and austere woman choose such a bland creature for a husband?"

"Probably to be able to continue being a characteristic and austere woman."

"Yes, but even if that were the case. A woman like her would grow frustrated with a dull husband after five minutes of marriage with him. She doesn't even seem quite comfortable with the enormous house that was attached to him."

"She is a complex woman, Watson. Not like the smiling chorus girls that you are used to. Her simple background is certainly the cause of her paradoxes. First the wish to flee from the squalor and then the guilt-ridden attempts to help others once she realises how fortunate she has become. Her husband was probably suitable in both endeavours. First as a promise, then as an aide. One half of her might be confused, but the other half knows exactly what it's doing. Yes, there is something quite Adler-esque about her."

130

"But do you think she was right to admit Julia Burton to her household?"

Holmes sucked eagerly on his cigarette.

"Ah! There we have another complex woman! It is interesting to compare the two, isn't it? Miss Julia probably has a poorer background than Mrs. Trubshawe, but the latter sees something of herself in the former. Miss Julia is impressionable and allows herself to be taken in by an unreliable young man. Of Mrs. Trubshawe's youthful mistakes we know nothing, but considering a meagre upbringing, we can hardly eliminate it, can we? In fact, when you contemplate the way she defended her maid in relating her story, it is most likely that she recognises her own younger self in Julia Burton's character. But the connection between these two women does not bring us closer to a solution, because Mrs. Trubshawe brought us here and so is not likely to be a culprit. And what took place between Julia Burton and *Mr* Trubshawe?"

I turned from my unpacking.

"Holmes! Surely, you do not suggest…"

"We must consider the clichés, Watson. They are tedious, I agree, but quite often, I'm afraid they are the truth. In this case, however, I doubt if the man of the house is quite up to scratch. He seems to be spending much too little time in the house, for one thing, so if he is betraying his wife he is likely to do it in London rather than here. But I doubt that too. He collects butterflies."

"Butterflies?"

"Muddy shoes and well-worn tweeds indicate an outdoors man, but there are no shooting trophies or guns in the house. And as we walked through the drawing room, I noticed that he had been using one of his pins for cleaning his pipe. And as you know, Watson, butterfly collecting and woman collecting do not go hand in hand."

The gong sounded. Holmes put out his cigarette on the wall panelling and sprung out of his chair.

"Dinner. I'm starving."

He hardly gave me time to change before pulling me out of my room. But despite all the hurry in getting down to dinner, he still had time to stop again by the velvet lampshade in the outer room, and study it for a few moments.

I awoke the next morning with a strange sensation that someone was watching me. I shifted in my bed and opened my eyes, only to see Sherlock Holmes, fully dressed, sitting right next to me, leaning forward impatiently in his chair like a child waiting for someone to come and play with him.

"For God's sake, Holmes," I moaned and covered my face with a pillow.

"Good morning, Watson. It's a wonderful day. The rain has stopped. The air is frosty and crisp. Would be a shame to miss a morning like this."

"What do you want, Holmes?"

"I want your company, my friend. There's much to do today. We have staff to question, and we need to inspect the grounds of the house. It was too dark when we arrived last night. I suggest we begin with that, to make the most of the morning."

"Is breakfast ready?"

"Not for another hour. Nothing like a breath of fresh air before breakfast, eh?"

"We will go out after breakfast," I declared and turned away from Holmes.

I must have gone back to sleep, for when I awoke again I had the clear feeling that I had been sleeping for at least another half hour. I opened my eyes and glanced to one side. Holmes was sitting there on the chair in the exact same posture as when I last looked at him.

"Have you been sitting there the whole time?" I asked.

"I'm waiting," he said.

"Can't you do something else until I have woken up?"

"No."

"No?"

"This was the next thing to do."

"What was?"

"Waking you up and going out with you."

"You're not trying very hard to wake me up, are you? Of course, staring at me for more than half an hour is quite effective in the long run."

"Well, I don't want to be rude."

"Rude!"

"I can wait. It's all right."

I drew a deep breath.

"Go and wait in the corridor. I will be with you in less than five minutes."

And so Holmes had his way, like usual. We went out of the house, which was only just waking up, and saw for the first time in daylight the impressive surroundings of the house. It was an appealing park of wide lawns and the occasional gnarled oak tree.

"The secretive visitor doesn't seem to have made an appearance since we arrived," said Holmes as we walked on the frosty grass, which crunched like biscuits under our feet.

"I wonder if he has anything to do with our mystery," said I.

"I'm positive that he does."

"Really? In what way?"

"I have a theory about it, but I won't say anything further until I have had it tested. When there has been a reply to my telegram, then I will know more."

"Telegram? What telegram?"

"I went to the village while you were still asleep and had a telegram sent."

"To whom? In what matter?"

Holmes waved off my questions.

"It is only an impulse. It probably won't amount to anything. Oh, look, a robin!"

Holmes rushed off across the grass. If he was unwilling to answer my questions or if he had simply been distracted was impossible to say.

"Then you've already been out here," I said.

"No no, I had no time to inspect the grounds. I just went to the village and back. For this I need an extra pair of eyes. Come along!"

We walked in a large circle around the house and paid particular attention to those areas around the driveway and by the pond where the strange man had been seen.

"Do you think this mysterious visitor and the blackguard who got Miss Burton fired from her previous job are the same man?" I asked Holmes.

"Of that I am almost certain," he replied. "She could, of course, have formed a similar entanglement out here, but there are virtually no people of that class around, and the ones that are, are employed in this household."

"But that man was sent to prison."

"More than six months ago. He could easily have been released since then. Or maybe he escaped."

"Do you think he has abducted poor Julia?"

"And then come back to this house for another one?"

"I see your point."

We had now walked in almost a complete circle around the house and had come to a place from where we could look up to Miss Burton's bedroom window. It was small and very high up, but one could just about make it out among the turrets and rooftops.

"Well," said Holmes, "I think we can rule out the possibility that she tied her sheets together and climbed out of her window."

We re-entered the house, and the warmth of it was welcome for, although the morning was bright and fresh, it was still very cold. We sat down to breakfast only to learn that Mr Trubshawe had already gone off to the City and that Mrs. Trubshawe was not feeling well and had chosen to have her breakfast in her room. Consequently, we felt that we had the house to ourselves, and so could organise the questioning of the staff according to our own preferences. We were assisted in this by the head butler, a big man with the face of a bulldog, called Mr Noakes, who I felt sure had been a most intimidating thug in his former life, but now had the demeanour of a domesticated bear. As he escorted us below stairs, he shared with us his own impressions of the vanished maid.

"I have nothing bad to say about Miss Julia, except that perhaps she was a bit shy and quite reluctant to talk to the other servants. She was doubtlessly Mrs. Trubshawe's current favourite, and she encouraged her drawing. Yes, Mrs. Trubshawe always has a special favourite among us, whom she devotes much of her time to, until she gets tired and finds another poor soul to rescue."

"Don't you get a bit overstaffed if your mistress feels the urge to employ all the lost souls she comes across?" I asked him.

"Oh yes. There are much too many of us, and have been for a few years now. Of course, now and then some of the maids and footmen find jobs elsewhere or go to London to make their fortune, but as it is, both me and Mrs. Keating, the housekeeper, have trouble finding things to do for everyone."

"Sounds like this house would be a haven for people in service who don't like to work too hard."

"Aye, it would be, if Mrs. Trubshawe would ever hire anyone with previous experience of service. With the way things are, word doesn't get round and every newcomer works hard to prove his or her worth. I've been here from the start and I've seen all sorts of people come and go. But on balance, I'd say Miss Julia belonged to the very best."

"Did anyone in the staff get acquainted with her more than the others?" asked Holmes.

Noakes scratched his patchy white beard.

"Well, all of the chambermaids tend to stick together, since they have the same duties. We currently have two more chambermaids, Janet and Daisy, who worked alongside Julia since she came."

"Very well. We shall start with them."

We had come to the kitchen quarters where people were busy preparing for lunch. It was strange after walking around the vast and empty house to be confronted with this chaos, but I suppose the invisibility of all these servants in the rest of the house was a measure of their good work, or of Mrs. Trubshawe's efficient schooling. We were given the servants' dining room at our disposal, and Mr Noakes went to fetch the two chambermaids. They entered the room within seconds, both looking pale and frightened, walking towards the large dining table pressed together like a pair of Siamese twins. Holmes kindly asked them to take a seat, and I almost thought they would sit down on the same chair. As they began talking, it seemed they were both a bit bewildered by Julia Burton, who, from their description, appeared to be infinitely more intelligent than the two of them together.

"She was funny when you wanted to talk to her," said Janet, "'cos she would want to talk about things that were a bit com- com- complicated."

"Yeah," agreed Daisy, "like death and love and those kinds of things. Right strange she was."

"I see," said Holmes. "And did she ever say anything that would make you think she was planning to disappear?"

"Not a word," said Daisy. "I thinks she was taken away, I does."

"Really? By whom?"

"Why, that bloke of hers, of course. Wot got her fired from her job."

Janet nodded in agreement.

It was quite clear to me that these two girls were very simpleminded, and if Julia had only a bit of intelligence, which I was starting to think she did, it would have been far from her mind to speak intimately with them. And as Holmes tried the rest of his questions on them, it became increasingly obvious that what help they could give us would only be by pure chance. They were thus dismissed and in came Mrs. Keating, the housekeeper. She was a dignified woman of about fifty, with jet black hair and a thin hawk nosed face, almost mirroring that of Holmes. As with all of these people, I couldn't help but wonder what her background was, and whether she too had been on the other side of the law.

"I shall not deny that I was sceptical when Mrs. Trubshawe hired Julia," she said. "She was an unusual sort of girl, not like the dim adolescents that get involved with the wrong sort of characters like other people step in puddles." (It was quite clear which girls she had in mind.) "No, Julia was bright and seemed to have learned from her experiences even though she was very young. I was told the story of the man she acquainted in London, but was always sure there was more to it than that. She played the part of the shy and awkward one, which is always a very clever part to play, because most people interpret it as lack of character or lack of intelligence, at best with a bit of primitive creativity to the mixture, but in reality it hides a calculating and conniving personality. I admit that I wavered in my interpretation of her, for most of the time she behaved perfectly and worked hard, but then again I know now that I was never really at ease when she was around. It was as if you would look away for two seconds and then she would be gone. And of course that was exactly what happened."

"So you foresaw this?" I inquired.

"Well, I won't pride myself with having known this would happen all along. But when it did happen, I was not surprised. And I can't really say why. It's as if she was never really here. And so vanishing was not much of an effort. Do you understand what I'm trying to say?"

I shook my head. Holmes nodded.

The questioning of the household staff did not make me much wiser, and Holmes was in a taciturn mood as we sat down to lunch with Mrs. Trubshawe. The lady of the house was most curious concerning our progress, but I felt I had to talk for both Holmes and me, and I had very little to say to her. Mrs. Trubshawe did not disappoint with her boldness, however, and turned directly to Holmes.

"You don't seem to have anything to say, Mr Holmes."

Holmes was gazing off into space and had no interest whatsoever in his plate. Only after a few seconds of silence did he flinch.

"Tell me, Mrs. Trubshawe, are you satisfied with the cleaning?"

Mrs. Trubshawe looked at Holmes, then at me, then at Holmes again.

"The what?"

"The cleaning. The cleaning of the house. I assume it is properly done?"

"Well, of course. I supervise it personally."

"And are you very particular about your possessions and what goes where and so on?"

"If you are concerned about my silverware I can assure you that the spoons are counted every week. As for the rest of the house, yes, it is very big, and I can't possibly be expected to keep an eye on every little detail, but I trust my staff and I would know if anything was not as it should be."

"Thank you, Mrs. Trubshawe, you have been most helpful." Holmes rose from his chair. "And now, if you will excuse me, I must go down to the village to see if there has been an answer to my cable."

He marched out of the room. Mrs. Trubshawe looked at me with a puzzled look, and I'm afraid I hardly looked less puzzled.

"What cable?" she said.

"I'm afraid he won't tell me."

"Is he always like this?"

"Oh no," I assured her, "sometimes he can be absolutely impossible."

Holmes was gone a couple of hours, and it was dark by the time he returned from the village. By then, Mr Trubshawe was also back from his office, and couldn't hide his disappointment at seeing Holmes gone without having solved the problem. However, the Trubshawes were soon to be placated. I was sitting down with them for tea in one of their drawing rooms, exchanging pleasantries on this trivial topic and that, a type of socialising that would have been quite impossible in the presence of Holmes. We could hear the front door open, and a few moments later Holmes strode into the room, brandishing a piece of paper above his head.

"We have our answer, gentlemen and lady, we have our answer!"

We all rose eagerly from our chairs, and demanded to be told the news. Holmes held up his palms.

"All in good time. If you will accompany me upstairs, I hope to have this mystery solved once and for all."

We looked at each other, mystified, but we followed, and realised soon enough, that Holmes was taking us to the vast cluttered room that we passed through on the way to our bedrooms. It looked just as it had the other times we had moved through it, and it seemed as strange to me now as the first time I saw it, both conspicuous in its extravagance and inconspicuous for being a room entirely without function through which one passed on one's way elsewhere. But the strangest thing about it was perhaps the curious little lamp on the table, the only source of light, condemning most of the room to an obscure and shadowy existence.

"Such an interesting room, don't you think," said Holmes as we were standing on the threshold. "Your uncle really had a taste for…exaggeration, Mr Trubshawe."

"Yes, well…" Mr Trubshawe mumbled.

Holmes walked forward and stopped in front of the lamp, which he had taken such interest in every time we had passed it.

"Doesn't it strike you as a bit odd that the room has all these treasures in it, and yet is only illuminated by a single table lamp?"

The Trubshawes looked at each other.

"Well, I suppose so," said Mrs. Trubshawe. "I haven't really thought about it. I don't think I had been up here for weeks before you came."

"Let's ask one of the staff," said Holmes, and pulled a bell rope on the wall.

Soon enough, Mr Noakes appeared in the doorway behind us, and Holmes asked him to fetch Janet or Daisy. We waited in silence a few seconds before one of them – I think it was Daisy, but it was always difficult for me to tell them apart – came into the room. She stepped up to us, assembled as we were around the lamp, and she could not quite hide a look of bewilderment.

"Is there something wrong, Daisy?" said Holmes.

"Well, no sir, only…"

"Only what?"

"Only that lampshade ain't supposed to be there."

"Really?"

"Oh no, sir. You see it makes the room all dark. Can't see a thing, can ya? No, I think that lampshade is supposed to be in the parlour next door."

"And where is the lampshade for this lamp?"

"It's not supposed to 'ave a lampshade, sir. Otherwise it's much too dark in 'ere."

She stepped up to the lamp and lifted off the big red velvet lampshade, revealing quite an attractive lamp underneath it, and one that did not need a lampshade to decorate it. But furthermore, when she removed the lampshade, we could see why there was only one lamp in the room —it now shone so bright that none other was needed. And as the room lit up, Mrs. Trubshawe let out a piercing scream. We looked at her, then in the direction she was pointing. She was pointing at a spot on the wall, just above where the lamp was standing. This area had been quite invisible to us before, but now as the light shone brighter, it was clear to us that a painting was missing. The pictures were hanging so close together all over the walls, that the disappearance of one became obvious immediately. In fact, had one painting been removed, it would have been impossible to hide the fact, unless the wall itself was hidden, and that, of course, could best be done by dimming the lights. That was when it all became clear to me.

"Good God, Holmes!" I couldn't help exclaiming.

"Yes. The curious placement of this lampshade on a lamp that didn't match it, caught my eye from the very beginning. This house is lavishly and profusely decorated, but all of it is done with the strictest attention to detail. Your uncle may have had delusions of grandeur, Mr Trubshawe, but there was also method in his madness. So much so that the displacement of a single lampshade becomes apparent to the observant eye."

"But the painting," said Mrs. Trubshawe. "The painting!" She was quite beside herself.

"The painting, I would venture, was a Vermeer. Much more valuable than any of the other objects in this house put together."

"How do you know, Holmes?" I asked.

"Miss Burton's sketches of it were expertly done, and when she had covered her walls almost exclusively with drawings of that particular picture, I would say that it was because she had her eye on it. She has probably conducted a bit of amateur art study with the help of books from your library, but one can hardly deny the brilliance of what she has pulled off."

"Pulled off?" said Mrs. Trubshawe. "You mean to imply it was she who stole it?"

"Oh most definitely. And I doubt that you will ever see her or the painting again. She will know how to turn it into hard currency."

"So you mean," said Mr Trubshawe, "that she removed the painting and then put a thick velvet lampshade on that lamp so that we wouldn't see it was missing?"

"Quite so. She knew that few people ever came her except the chambermaids who turned up this light every afternoon. Luckily for Julia, Daisy wasn't the one who had this task, or she would have noticed it. But the lampshade was just a precaution that would give her a head start, at best. Sooner or later, the theft was going to be discovered."

"But if this is the case," I said, "then it would be easy to find her. A little girl with a large canvas under her arm?"

"Ah, but she thought of that too. She had a large trunk packed and ready underneath her bed. You saw the traces it had left in the dust yourselves. And it was large enough to contain the painting."

"I can't believe it," said Mrs. Trubshawe. "Not our Julia."

I would have liked to ponder about what kind of a girl this Julia Burton really was, but we were interrupted by Daisy, who had suddenly run up to the window and was pointing out.

"There 'e is!" she cried. "The strange man! Out there, on the lawn!"

Holmes and I stepped up to the window, and saw a large silhouette moving among the trees.

"Quickly, Watson! We mustn't let him get away!"

Holmes ran towards the door, and I followed. We rushed down the main stairs and out of the front door. Holmes was taking enormous strides with his long spidery legs and I could only just keep up with him. I was still running down the front steps when Holmes caught hold of the man by his coat. He tried to wriggle out of it, and had nearly succeeded when I came to the scene and tripped him over so that Holmes could sit on him and pull his arms around his back.

"It's no use," he said. "Just come with us into the house and we will have the police here in a few minutes."

"Never!" screamed the big man. "That bitch! I'll cut her bleedin' throat!"

"Temper," said Holmes calmly, sitting on top of him as though it were the most normal thing in the world.

It took a bit of struggle to get him into the house, and only with the help of Mr Noakes did we finally manage it. Thankfully, Noakes was at least as big as this man, which helped us to pacify the intruder considerably. Ten minutes later, he was sitting in a sofa in front of the roaring fire of the Trubshawes' sitting room, his hands tied behind his back.

"What is your name?" asked Holmes.

The man did not reply.

"Very well," continued Holmes, "we can easily find it out for ourselves. I take it that you are the same man who terrorised Miss Burton in London and managed to get her dismissed from her household there?"

"Julia Burton is a scheming wench!" said the man.

Mrs. Trubshawe looked at him with an anxious expression, looking very concerned about the future of the sofa on which he sat.

"Yes, I'm sure she is," agreed Holmes. "But you have to admire her ingenuity. I trust that you planned the theft together?"

"Where is she?" roared the man. "I demand to see her!"

I realised that he wasn't aware that she was gone. That was of course the reason why he had been skulking around the house these past few days.

"She's gone," said Holmes.

The man's fury increased and he writhed about on the sofa like some chained animal.

"I knew it! She took off with the loot!"

The more he spoke, the more he incriminated himself, and soon he didn't seem to care anymore. He told everything.

"I came here a week ago. I've been looking for Julia everywhere since they released me. She's mine, you see. She's said so herself. And then someone told me about a big house outside of Pangbourne where people of our sort go when they want to make a decent living. I came here, I think, both to take her with me and to make her pay for what she'd done to me."

"Blasted scoundrel," I couldn't help but hiss through my teeth. Holmes silenced me with a discreet gesture.

"And I managed to find her here," continued the man, "and she actually seemed glad to see me. But she said we couldn't run away together just yet, cos she had a plan. She had found a painting in this house that she thought was valuable, and so if we could take it with us and then sell it, our fortune would be made. She told me to wait for her by the pond on Thursday, but she never came. I waited again the next day, and continued to come here every day. Tonight I came here to knock on the door and demand to see her. Didn't know I was too late."

"In fact," said Holmes, "she'd been gone two days already by Thursday. She tricked you. And took the painting with her."

The man's anger gave way to a solemn and, thank God, quiet sulk. He appeared to me every inch the common half-witted small-time criminal, and it would have been no stretch for Julia Burton to deceive him.

"So where is Julia Burton?" I asked myself. "It must be possible to trace her."

Holmes smiled gently at me.

"That, my good doctor, is just what my telegram this morning was about. It was addressed to Inspector Lestrade, asking him to find out whether a girl of Julia Burton's description had boarded any ship out of the country in the last few days."

"And you seemed quite pleased with his reply."

Holmes nodded. But Mrs. Trubshawe looked anxious.

"I can't quite believe that poor Julia has done this. I knew her so well. We actually came quite close to each other during her time here. I mean, all this is purely circumstantial. How can you be so sure that she has done what you claim, and escaped from the country?"

"The evidence is circumstantial," said Holmes. "I grant you that. But taken together, it points to an obvious conclusion."

"But how could you possibly trace her among all the hundreds of people boarding ships in this country?"

"Actually, it turned out to be much easier than I had thought. If you look at this telegram that I received from Inspector Lestrade, you will see the name under which a young lady boarded a steamship bound for Calais two days ago."

Mrs. Trubshawe took the paper, held it up to her face and read aloud:

"'Olivia Trubshawe.'" She looked up at us with bulging eyes. Then – and I cannot blame her – she fainted.

Thus it was that the conclusion of the Julia Burton case came to Sherlock Holmes' attention through the curious placement of a velvet lampshade. The stolen Vermeer was searched by police forces on two continents, but was never recovered, thought to have been sold secretly to a wealthy buyer of dubious scruples. The Trubshawes chose not to make any charges against their uninvited male intruder, and he never pestered them again. Mrs. Trubshawe, as far as I know, did not cease her practice of hiring reformed criminals and outcasts to her household, and I still admire her brave initiative, although I suspect that the experience of Julia Burton added an insight into the unpredictability of human nature, well-needed for someone engaged in philanthropic activities. I sometimes wonder whether Julia's choice to register as a passenger under her former employer's name was meant as a tribute to her saviour, or as a scornful rebuke to what she perceived as a blue-eyed aristocrat. Whatever the case, I suppose the gesture worked as a constructive lesson to she who I will always consider to be a laudable woman.

The Adventure of the Missing Mudlark

One afternoon in September, as I was returning home after taking lunch at my club, I saw a shady character lurking outside the door of 221B. It was a middle-aged man, pacing up and down the pavement as did many of our prospective clients probably unsure of whether or not he should pay my friend Sherlock Holmes a visit. In this case, however, the man's restlessness was also likely to do with the fact that he felt out of place on a West End street, for he was dressed in the shabbiest of clothes, a brown cloth cap with a matching jacket, frayed around the cuffs and lapels, a baggy pair of trousers, and shoes that looked like they had walked from the far end of the world to come here. I walked past him up to our door, and I saw him react, and, with hesitation, approach me.

"Are you a friend of Mr 'Olmes?" he asked.

"I am his associate," I conceded. "Dr John Watson."

"Then I would very much like to ask for your assistance in an urgent matter." He paused, looking worried. "Does your Mr 'Olmes charge a lot?"

I stepped towards him and smiled as disarmingly as I could.

"Mr Holmes tries to help people from all walks of life, and the rewards he gets from those who have the ability to remunerate him handsomely allow him to take on clients of lesser means."

He seemed to struggle to follow what I was saying, but realised that it was encouraging news, and as I opened the door, he walked past me into the hallway. I showed him up the stairs to our sitting room, where we found Holmes bowed over the table, absorbed in the study of a large coloured map which he had spread out so as to create a makeshift tablecloth. He didn't look up when we entered.

"Holmes, I have a client for you," I said.

"Mmhmm," he replied, without taking his eyes from the magnifying glass in his hand, which he slowly traced across the map.

I walked up to him, feeling slightly embarrassed in front of the visitor I had so enthusiastically persuaded to come in.

"What are you doing?"

"Ha!" Holmes exclaimed to himself. "Ill-informed, quite ill-informed."

"Holmes?"

He finally noticed me.

"Ah, Watson. Have a look at this. I just bought it at the stationer's down the road. They call it the London poverty map. It was recently published, and has been compiled by a statistician by the name of Booth. At first, I thought it quite ingenious. You see, he's had the idea of charting the degree of poverty and criminality in every London street, and then colouring each street on the map according to a classification, so a street that is coloured in black will belong to the poorest and vilest of streets, while a yellow street is a wealthy upper-class street. And in between there's a scale, from dark blue and blue to pink and bright red."

"Indeed? Well, that's fascinating, isn't it?"

"That is exactly what one would think! But this Booth fellow and his co-workers, although they have walked down each and every street that they describe, seem somehow unable to break free from their armchair opinions and petty bourgeois prejudice! From just a brief glance at this map, I can see several streets that they have completely misinterpreted and features that have passed them by unnoticed. For instance, the den of prostitutes and pickpockets in Shoreditch High Street has completely escaped their attention allowing them to classify the whole of that street as "well-to-do". The cause of all their omissions is their method, namely walking the streets accompanied by local policemen, either constables or superintendents, and taking the officers' insights into the local streetlife at face value, when it is fairly obvious to everyone with even a slight knowledge of London streetlife that the awareness of the London police forces encompasses only a fraction of what really goes on in this city!"

Holmes fell back laughing, at which point he noticed the presence of our visitor. Instead of becoming self-conscious and embarrassed, however, he allowed his enthusiasm for the map to transgress into his greeting of the confused man.

"Watson, why didn't you tell me we had a visitor? Good afternoon, sir, please come in, draw up a chair! I am Sherlock Holmes."

"Walter Shadmore," replied the man.

"Mr Shadmore? All the way from Wapping, I see? Your way of tying that bright-coloured neckerchief of yours is quite distinctive of the costermongers of that particular area. Have a seat. You too, Watson, I might need an extra pair of ears for this one. Now then, Mr Shadmore, how may we help you?"

Shadmore, sitting uneasily on the rickety chair, eyed us for a moment, then gave way to his urgency.

"Mr 'Olmes, you must 'elp me. My little boy Roger is gone missin'. 'E's been gone these four days now and I don't know what to do. 'E's just twelve years old, and Lor' knows what mess 'e's got himself involved in!"

Holmes raised a hand.

"Please, Mr Shadmore, try to keep calm and tell us everything from the beginning."

"Well then. We live in Wapping, in a small back street just up the shore from the wharves of the Ceylon Tea-Trading Company. I make my living sometimes as a street seller, but mostly as a rag-and-bone man, making rounds every morning to find discarded bits of bone, cloth, rag, paper, you name it, which I then keep in a cellar storage in the house where we live. It is a rough life, but I make a decent living, especially when you consider it's just me and the boy. 'Is mother died three years ago – 'er lungs packed in after a lifetime working at a charcoal factory up North – and since then we've had to make do. And it was 'e who insisted that 'e should contribute to the 'ousehold by working. 'E's 'ad a dozen jobs, but since a year back 'e's become somethin' of a professional mudlark, goin' about the Thames foreshore, scavenging a bit of this and a bit of that, and quite often findin' things 'e can sell for a good profit. There's a whole gang of 'em out Wapping way, goin' down Wapping steps together, darting back and forth around the boats. I wouldn't recommend it to young lads, gentlemen, that I would not, but since Roger started mudlarkin' 'e's found a purpose, like, and the lads 'e goes out with are good lads, all of 'em. I sometimes don't see 'im all day, but 'e always comes home before dark. Well, until Tuesday. Now, after the first day, I was thinkin' 'e'd gone home with one of the other boys, and so I told myself not to worry. But the next night, I became anxious, and I went around lookin' for 'im. I went round to the parents of the other mudlarkin' boys but none of them knew where 'e'd gone. The boys are always reluctant to speak of their goings-on. It's like a little secret club for them, you know, with their boyish ways and all, and so it can be difficult tryin' to get somethin' out of 'em, but all the boys I talked to claimed not to have seen Roger since Tuesday. They're good lads, but some of 'em I just don't like the look of. I'm sure there are factions and rivalries between the various gangs, and you know how lads that age can bully each other. It's 'orrible. Well, I've been out lookin' again, and have even got help from some of the neighbours, but there's been no sign of Roger now for four days. And we're lawabidin' people, but you see, goin' to the police about these things, it can be quite a problem."

There had been so many things in this man's story that I had found appalling and tragic, and I did not envy Holmes' position in questioning this man, for I would not know where to begin trying to understand the logic and meaning of the world in which he lived. It was therefore perhaps not surprising that I found Holmes' first question unexpected.

"What is the name of the back street where you and your son live?"

Shadmore looked as if being asked the most personal thing imaginable.

"Uh, it's called Pennington Close."

"Ah yes, I know it well. It is a hobby of mine to have an exact knowledge of London, so let's see. It is quite a long and narrow alleyway, is it not, but with only a few features. At the top of it is the public house on the corner, 'The Boatswain' if I am not mistaken, then there is the meat-packing warehouse, the used-clothes dealer, two opposing entrances to court dwellings where I assume you live, and then a few seedy houses, one of which contains an opium den if my suspicions are correct, and then it's all tea-trading warehouses down to the riverfront."

"By Jove, sir, you're quite correct!"

"Good! Then we know where we are." Holmes leaned across the map on the table. "Let us, for the sake of curiosity, see how Mr Booth categorises this street. Yes, it's purple, meaning 'Mixed. Some comfortable, some poor.' Yes, as usual, it seems, Mr Booth, in his admirable strive for general conclusions, gets it all wrong. There is nothing so dangerous as the will to generalise, Watson, mark my words! Now, Mr Shadmore, have you made inquiries in your area apart from the families of the other mudlarks?"

"Well, as I said, I've been lookin' about. I talked to a few of the warehousemen and maybe a sailor or two, but when the subject is mudlarkin' you really have to be careful who you talk to, and it's not easy to get any information out of people because most of 'em are quite prejudiced."

"I see. And I take it you yourself would have a limited knowledge of any other acquaintances that your son would make while doing his rounds?"

"I'm afraid so, Mr 'Olmes. Of course, there are people in the neighbourhood that I have my eye on, people who are not quite straight, if you take my meaning."

"Go on."

"Well, your suspicions are quite correct in that there is an opium den further down the street, and the man who keeps it is a weird and secretive character, Mr Fon is the name. He is most disliked by all who live there, and it is generally accepted that he has other criminal dealings as well, though no one knows by first-hand knowledge. And since mudlarkin' is quite a provocative business to some, I wouldn't hold it above some of the warehousemen to get their back on a mudlark if they suspected 'im of stealin' or some such thing."

"Yes, there are many possible scenarios. Well, Mr Shadmore, your case interests me exceedingly, if only as an opportunity to disprove some of the theories of Mr Booth. I don't think I will need any more information from you at the moment. I will make some inquiries, and quite possibly we will encounter one another in your neighbourhood shortly. I cannot promise you anything, but the mystery has many potential leads and it would be strange if I came up with nothing."

Shadmore rose from his chair.

"I thank you, Mr 'Olmes. 'Ow soon can I expect to 'ear from you?"

"Before tomorrow afternoon, I'm sure."

I was quite taken aback by Holmes' self-confidence in what I perceived to be quite an obscure business with many possible dead ends. He showed Shadmore to the door, when our client suddenly stopped in his tracks and turned around.

"Oh, I almost forgot. It might be nothin' of course…"

"Please tell," requested Holmes.

"As I was nosin' around, I found this in the sand of the foreshore. Roger found it one day, and 'e's kept it ever since as a sort of lucky charm."

Shadmore dropped the object into the palm of Holmes' hand.

"Hm! It's a Roman coin," he swiftly observed. "At least fifteen hundred years old. Where exactly did you find it?"

"Just about twenty yards west of the bottom of Pennington Close steps at low tide. It's the only thing of Roger's I've found."

Holmes rested a reassuring hand on Shadmore's shoulder and opened the door for him. When he had closed it behind him, he swung round and tossed the valuable coin in the air.

"Well, well, what fascinating little secrets London still holds."

"Holmes," I said. "This case is quite intriguing. Who would think that such remarkable things still existed in our modern capital. Mudlarks. Rag-and-bone men. It's the stuff of Mayhew!"

"Yes. This is a most serious business but at the same time, a golden opportunity to do some scientific research into the underworld of this city."

"Holmes, you are a calculating and cold machine! How can you speak of research when a boy's life is at stake?"

"Hm! Well, we can't say anything substantial at this point, but it is my experience that thirteen-year old boys in the world of Walter and Roger Shadmore are more grown-up than thirteen-year old boys elsewhere. After all, the father waited four days before consulting us, and that is probably more than most parents would do, and not out of a lack of sensibility, but because they trust in their children and allow them more freedom than parents of the well-to-do. But Mr Shadmore's anxiety suggests that he fears something, and he did not share his worst fears with us. Watson! Will you take down the index volume from the bookcase and see what we have on mudlarks in our commonplace books?"

I did as he asked, leafing through entries of mashers, match girls, mendicants and mourning warehouses before finding what he asked for. The clippings and references filled several pages, and I took the liberty of quoting at length from a few of them:

"'These poor creatures are certainly about the most deplorable in their appearance of any I have met with in the course of my inquiries,'" I read. "'They may be seen of all ages, from mere childhood to positive decrepitude, crawling among the barges at the various wharfs along the river; it cannot be said that they are clad in rags, for they are scarcely half covered by the tattered indescribable things that serve them for clothing; their bodies are grimed with the foul soil of the river, and their torn garments stiffened up like boards with dirt of every possible description. The mudlarks collect whatever they happen to find, such as coals, bits of old iron, rope, bones, and copper nails that drop from ships while lying or repairing along shore. The coals that the mud-larks find, they sell to the poor people of the neighbourhood. The iron and bones and rope and copper nails which they collect, they sell at the rag-shops.'"

I looked up from the volume, but noticed that Holmes was making a disgruntled face at the words.

"I can understand if the account pains you," I said.

"It pains me no end, Watson! But it is not the contents and the harsh living conditions of the mudlark that pain me, but the sentimental and pompous language of the journalist. Oh, that we shall soon be spared of conceited and self-righteous journalist missionaries! No, direct experience is the only remedy against the distorted images of the popular press."

And with these words, he rushed into his adjacent bedroom while removing his dressing gown. He stopped in the doorway, a sinister smile playing on his face.

"I shall be going out for a while, Watson. Don't expect me back until late this evening, at the earliest."

"I will come with you," I said, rising from my chair.

"No no, we will come to that. For the time being, a discreet and solitary assessment is the right step. We must approach this problem softly, Watson, for make no mistake: we are moving in the lowest and most desperate circles here, and we must be prepared to suspend our regular sense of morality and decency if we want to understand the people of this world. But I will tell you this: a boy clever enough to find a rare Roman coin at the bottom of a river has surprisingly few enemies in that world."

He smiled again, then disappeared into his room.

It was dark by the time I saw Holmes again. Before he went out, he had spent almost half an hour disguising himself into what, from the brief glance I caught of it as he hurried out of the house, I assumed to be a drunken sailor or whatnot. When he returned, well after eleven o'clock in the evening, I had a chance to admire the get-up undisturbed. He was wearing a greasy peaked cap, had a spotted handkerchief around his naked neck and a black double-breasted pea coat. He had covered his face in a pair of curly grey side-whiskers with matching bushy eyebrows, and as he came in and sat down beside me by the fireplace with his regular bearing and body language, the contrast was almost comical. Noticing my amused look, he removed the facial hair and the hat, then warmed his hands by the fire.

"What a long day it has been!" he groaned. "Long and cold. The way this September weather is developing, we shall have the autumn over us in the matter of a few days."

I quickly slammed shut my book and threw it aside.

"Oh don't keep me waiting, Holmes! You've been out and about and I demand to know what you have learned since this afternoon."

Holmes sniggered like a cunning jester.

"Have no fear, doctor. You shall have all the details, for I need your opinion on some aspects. But first, allow me to remove this coat, replace it with my dressing gown and then fill my pipe, for I am in need of comfort after my escapades."

He rose, and after a few minutes he was back in his chair, looking his usual self, and beginning his narrative with his eyes resting on the logs in the fire.

"The vicinity of Pennington Close is a vile and disreputable area, but not without its points of interest for a student of the shadier aspects of London life. It is located in the Shadwell end of Wapping, and you might easily miss it unless you were looking for it, since its entrance is partially boarded up with just a small door in the planking. In fact, it is most readily accessed through the public house, which has one entrance in Wapping High Street and one in Pennington Close. My first stop was of course this pub, which serves as a sort of gateway between the public world of the high street and the semi-public world of the close. Since it was still quite early when I came there, the taproom was almost empty apart from a few drunken loners. I struck up a conversation with the landlord, and I managed to steer the talk towards the topic of the missing mudlark without too much of an effort. He told me that Shadmore had been there several times inquiring about his boy, asking each and every visitor but to no avail.

"'He's startin' to become somethin' of a nuisance in this neighbour'ood', he said. 'But I think 'e should demand an answer from those other lads what go around the docks mudlarkin', cos there's a lot of loyalty and honour among them. And if one of 'em goes missin' I don't think they would squeal in the first place, not even to a parent.'

"'You mean the boy doesn't want to be found?' I asked him.

"'I mean when yer a mudlark, you subscribe to certain rules, like. We shouldn't assume that they think like we do.'

"'When did you last see the Shadmore boy?'

161

"'Eh, guvnor, you're startin' to sound like the p'lice! As a matter of fact, the boy always comes by the pub when 'e's on 'is way to work, so to speak, cos 'e goes down to the riverbed via Wapping steps, and not the steps at the bottom of Pennington Close. And 'e comes by the pub in the early hours of the mornin' when I'm busy takin' in groceries to the larder, so we usually greet one another. But on Tuesday I never saw 'im, and I 'aven't seen 'im since then!'

"I took note of the landlord's remark, but knew that I needed more information before I could make something out of it, so I paid for my cider and left the pub through the Pennington Close entrance.

"On the face of it, this narrow back street is quite similar to the main streets of Wapping. There are sailors lounging up against the brick walls, porters and warehousemen carrying crates and sacks and shouting over the heads of passersby, children darting in and out of the crowds as if this was their playground, and the occasional destitute beggar generally ignored by all and sundry. I took a slow-paced walk down the street, trying to be as inconspicuous as possible without moving along too quickly to be able to observe. I found the courtyard where Shadmore has his home and shop, and this is quite a welcoming part of the street, at least in comparison with what the rest of it has to offer. There is laundry hanging from the windows, and little assemblies of women gossip in the doorways. It was here that I ran into a couple of boys, who almost pushed me over as they came running round a corner. I caught hold of them, pretending to be angry, and judging from how they looked at me it must have been quite an effective performance, but then I produced some toffee

162

from my inner pocket – always handy when you are dealing with minors – and managed to gain their confidence. I told them I was thinking about going into the mudlarking business and said that I had been told to talk to the 'Pennington Close boys'. Their reply to this was expected.

"'Who told you?' they asked with considerable suspicion, while chewing away at their sweets.

"I made up some story of how their exploits were more famous than they thought, taking the opportunity to flatter them, and as I spoke I saw how they were gradually taken in by my admiring attitude. It wasn't long before I could question them about their work in order to acquire an insight into their world. It seems that they go out very early in the morning, and they don't have to stray too far from their place of residence as that particular part of the river offers an abundance of debris dropped or thrown from the numerous ships that pass there daily, not to mention the workshops and warehouses that line that stretch of the river on both sides. They told me how they might even find luxury items such as fine porcelain or jewellery that has been dropped upriver and is then pulled out with the tide. It's interesting to note, don't you think, Watson, that the Thames is regulated by the tide, which technically makes the Thames shore a coastline all the way up to Teddington lock!

Anyway, since I had established myself as a sort of co-conspirator in my ambition to take up mudlarking, I found it not too difficult to ask them about possible hindrances to the job. They managed to convey to me the great advantage being a child means in their business, mainly due to the ability to get into cramped spaces underneath piers and docks, but also to be able to disappear quickly if the enemy is approaching. Exactly who the enemy is, they were reluctant to elaborate upon, but quite soon they were talking about people in the neighbourhood that they disliked, such as the landlord of The Boatswain, who has it in his mind that these boys steal things from his larder. After a while, it seemed to me that the boys look upon virtually all adults of the neighbourhood as the enemy, and I do believe it is part of their worldview and autonomy to distance themselves from the grown-up world. I could not gain any information on possible rivalries among the mudlarks, but one of the dwellers of Pennington Close emerged as a distinctly dangerous presence. As soon as our talk drifted into mentioning the infamous opium den further down the close, the boys avoided saying the name of its owner.

"'We don't go near 'im,' said one boy. ''E's a monster!'

"'That's right,' agreed the other, 'a right monster 'e is. With 'is long fingernails like claws and the eyes of a cat. They say 'e eats children for breakfast!'

"I secretly found their conception of this Mr Fon a bit amusing, but told myself that their fear must have a foundation in experience, and tried to get them to say more about him, but my questions only served to undermine the trust I had managed to build between us, and the boys were now eager to conclude our discourse.

"Letting them continue on their way, I retraced my footsteps out of the courtyard. Darkness was falling, and the street was now almost empty of people, apart from one bulky figure walking towards me. As it stepped into the light from an overhead window, I could see that it was the imposing and, to be honest, reassuring presence of a police constable on the beat. His words to me were just as telling to his identity as his uniform.

"'Oi! You there! Why are you hangin' about like that?' he said like a sergeant major to a private.

"I decided to reveal my true identity to him, as I thought it might make him more helpful to me, and more inclined to speak to me in confidence. Explaining who I was took a few minutes, but luckily he had heard of me and my methods, and soon we were talking like colleagues. He was a jolly and likeable fellow, with a beaming smile, big red cheeks and a small curled moustache. The state of his uniform revealed, however, a meticulous and orderly personality, and his shining buttons and tight skin gloves put me in mind of a former army man. He introduced himself as PC Archibald Morris of the Thames Division. I asked him about his beat and, as is often the way with patrolling officers in want of company, he took every opportunity to talk at length about his undertakings.

"'It's a decent enough area, I suppose. There used to be quite a bit of drunkenness among the poorest dwellers, parents getting their children to fetch beer from the pubs, that sort of thing, but nowadays a lot of people have moved out, and there are wharves and warehouses where there used to be dwellings. No, what we really have a problem with is the quite substantial immigrant population. There are Italians and Greeks, but also quite a bit of Africans and Chinese. These last groups are mainly limited to sailors and the like, and they seldom stay for long, but since there is a steady stream of sailors coming and going, some of 'em have to settle to meet their everyday needs. So now we have public houses catering for Egyptians and Mediterraneans, there's a Chinese shop on the main road and a couple of lodging houses specialising on foreign sailors.'

"'What about opium dens?' I asked.

"'No, no opium dens', he replied with a condescending smile. 'No, most of the people here come and go without much trouble, and there is little criminality among them. No, the main trouble is the skirmishes that sometimes come about between the immigrants and the English population. At one point there was a full riot when people in the neighbourhood suspected a local Chinaman of molesting a small child. It turned out the child had been making up the allegations all along, but you can never really lay to rest the sense of unease between the various groups. Why, just the other day we had a pub brawl between an Italian gentleman and a Spanish sailor, which ended in the latter one getting his nose cut off.'

"'I see. But what about the mudlarks? I know street boys like that easily form gangs and fight wars.'

"'We've had our fair share of that too, yes. Oh, they're a vicious lot when it comes down to it. Every faction has its leader and you know how young boys are when they feel the power like that, like bleedin' tyrants, they are, and any boy who gets in the way, well, I shudder to think about it.'

"'What do you think they would be capable of?'

"'Oh, horrible things, but not murder or something like that. They would beat him up or chase him away from the area, nothing more.'

166

"'Interesting. You seem to be quite well-informed, Mr Morris. But are there any areas around here that the police have difficulties keeping under surveillance?'

"Morris shook his head immediately.

"'No. You mustn't underestimate the Metropolitan Police, sir. We are very thorough. As a matter of fact, I recently had the opportunity to escort a gentleman round my beat who was attached to Mr Booth's poverty survey, if you are familiar with it.'

"I replied in the affirmative, and gathered from the man's body language that he was very proud of the deed, and that he saw it as an immortalisation of his work as a constable. I have encountered dozens of constables like PC Morris, Watson. The police forces of London engender in some of their men a sort of occupational pride which, I am sorry to say, much too often gets in the way of the exactitude of their work. PC Morris had been going about this beat for several years, and it would never occur to him that he may have missed anything, and his confidence as an authority on this particular area of Wapping is so conceited that new information is seldom absorbed. He thinks he knows everything there is to know, an attitude which is always an effective remedy against acquiring new knowledge. I therefore realised that PC Morris was not the best potential source of information on what went on in Pennington Close, and let him continue on his beat.

"I lingered in the close, examining the rest of it down to the river, where it ended in steps disappearing into the water. This area was characterised by the wharves on either side, but now as night was falling, it changed, the daily doings of the workers drawing to a close, and being supplanted by a silent but ominous atmosphere. It was then that I noticed a faint red light coming from within a passageway leading into the court of one of the warehouses. I know through second-hand accounts that Pennington Close is the location of one of London's oldest opium dens, Watson, but I have never visited the place myself until today. Stepping towards the passageway, I could, halfway through, make out a low arched doorway with a narrow flight of steps leading down to a cellar entrance. Above the doorway hung a Chinese lamp of thin red paper on a nail driven into the mortar between the bricks. Going down the steps, I gathered that this establishment probably owed its relatively long life to a great amount of secrecy and candour, which would mean that I could not simply go in. Someone would ask me for a password or a name, and I did not know what answer I would give. I searched my memory for something, some word or act, that would make up the most likely ritual for gaining entrance to a place like this, but I couldn't think of anything. Then, when the door opened and I saw a young Chinese man clad in black looking at me with an indifferent face, I forced myself to act as if I was a regular customer. I bowed gently, a gesture that he responded to, and then I said:

"'Ān de měngshì xī shǒu sìfāng.'

"It is a line from an ancient poem written by the first Chinese emperor of the Han people. Since I know that a majority of the Chinese population in London belongs to the Han Chinese, I guessed that quoting from this well-known piece of literature would hardly worsen my chances of being let inside. And, as if through a miracle, the young man smiled and stepped aside, letting me in. I have no idea of whether what I said was the password or just something so unlikely that the Chinaman was all too delighted to hear it, but it did the trick, and I had gained admittance to London's most notorious opium den.

"You will remember The Bar of Gold in Upper Swandam Lane, and our experiences in that vile den, Watson, but let me tell you, that place seems like the Athenaeum Club in comparison with the den at Pennington Close. First of all, it was housed in a deserted cellar with an arched ceiling so low that I had to walk around folded in two. All over the floor, motionless bodies were lying scattered and the atmosphere of evaporated opium was so thick that one would hardly need to pay for a pipe to get one's fill of the drug. The Bar of Gold was a disreputable establishment, but at least one fit for the likes of Isa Whitney and Neville St Clair, but this place obviously catered to a circle of customers a bit lower down the social scale.

"As I walked on, the ceiling became higher, and I came to a corner where a big robust Chinese desk had been placed as a sort of makeshift counter. Being finally able to straighten my back, I had the opportunity to look about and orientate myself. I could conclude that the whole place encompassed only a few square feet, and there were no other entries or exits apart from the door through which I had entered, and another door behind the desk. The customers on the floor were all grown men and women and there was no place in the room I had entered where a child could have been hidden. Naturally, my attention was drawn to the back door. At the desk, another Chinese gentleman was seated. He had a long dark moustache and his face was thin and emaciated, but smiling. I approached him and asked to speak to Mr Fon.

"'And who shall I say wants to see him?' asked the Chinaman.

"'Sherlock Holmes,' I said.

"I surmised that revealing my true identity would be just as effective as trying to infiltrate the place via an assumed one, but quicker. The man had evidently heard of me, and he disclosed what I had already appreciated, that he was Mr Fon.

"'It is an honour to meet so distinguished a man as yourself, Mr Holmes,' he said. 'What brings you to my establishment? Am I to understand that you are my nemesis and that you have taken it upon yourself to bring about my downfall?'

"'I have no interest in your affairs, Fon, and my purpose is not to work against you. I only ask for your assistance in a business that has occurred on your doorstep.'

"'Ah, I think I know to what you are referring, Mr Holmes. The little boy who has gone missing? Yes, I have eyes and ears all over this district and I know everything that goes on around here.' Then his face changed, looking quite sad. 'But I am sorry to say that this mystery eludes even me. I know about the mudlark boys, of course, and some of them even come in here sometimes, but this particular boy I have never seen in here. I have spoken to one of the foremen at the warehouse, Mr Boyd, and he was earnestly perplexed by the disappearance. Mr Boyd knows everything that goes on in the docks and he keeps a meticulous record of the ships on this stretch of the river, but none of the men he had spoken to had seen the boy, neither on any of the ships that were anchored by Pennington Close that day, or on the Thames foreshore at low tide.'

"'Excuse me, master.'

"This was the young man at the door who had evidently overheard our discussion and felt obliged to interrupt. We both turned to him.

"'I saw the boy on Tuesday,' he said. 'I was standing by the river steps early in the morning having a smoke, when he came past me. I'm sure it was him because in time I have learned to recognised these boys. But I couldn't stop him, because he was running at a furious speed, coming from up the street, rushing down the steps and disappearing round the corner at the bottom. But what made me look up was the way he was running. So rapidly. Almost as if he was running for his life.'

"'Did you notice anything else about him?' I asked.

"'No. Only his hurry. There were no other boys with him, or in the street. There was quite a bustle around the docks and wharves at that time, but the boy managed to pass through the crowd very effectively.'

"Mr Fon was nodding slowly.

"'He is quite a bright young man, don't you think, Mr Holmes? Chang is my oldest son. He went to Winchester, you know!'

"'His manner of speech betrays that,' I said.

"What Mr Fon's son and doorman had said was of course of vital importance, and I thanked both of them for helping me. Mr Fon wished me good luck."

"But Holmes!" I could remain silent no longer. "Do you mean to tell me you walked out of there with gratitude?"

"What else could I do?"

"Well, at least make some indication that you frowned upon their business! My God, the man even admitted to supplying opium to young children! Surely this cannot pass us unremedied!"

"Watson, this really isn't the time to instigate a raid on opium dens. Mr Fon and his son were very helpful to me. It is not our place to do police work where the police have failed. Criminals endeavour to hide their businesses from the police and the police endeavour to uncover those hidden businesses. But if the criminals' hiding is better done than the police's act of uncovering, then my sympathy is with the criminals. Let the cleverest man win!"

"Holmes, I sometimes think you are a nihilist!"

He quivered with laughter.

"Let us just say I am a hound on the scent without concern for juicy bones along the way! But we must keep our focus on the business at hand. The case is an intriguing one, Watson, and it is fascinating to note that the closed location of a narrow Wapping back street dictates an investigation that could have led us anywhere in this great city of ours."

"But what happened during the rest of your adventure? I demand to be told everything."

"Oh, the rest of it was taken up by the mere filling up of gaps in the weave. I inspected the steps leading down to the river, but there was little I could do as the tide had come in, and the street was insufficiently lit for an investigation in the pitch dark of midnight. That is why I have come back to you and why we must be up as early as we can tomorrow morning and conclude this case before it is too late!"

"But I don't understand. You have the solution already?"

"There are still a few points which need clearing up, but the hypothesis is a strong one."

"Won't you share it with me?"

"Well, the whole thing is quite simple. The only things we know are that the landlord of The Boatswain didn't see young Roger on the morning of the Tuesday, and that Mr Fon's son did see him."

"Right. Which would mean that instead of walking up the street, he ran down it."

"Exactly! And that, I am convinced, is the key to the whole mystery. He always went to Wapping Steps, but on that particular day, something made him go the other way! And it must have been something terrifying, for why would he be running for his life otherwise? This was his street, his neighbourhood. Why run?"

"What do you think it was, Holmes?"

"It is too soon to say. I need to test my theory in the morning before I put words to my suspicions."

"But he can't have run very far. That Boyd character, the friend of Mr Fon, was sure he hadn't been seen on the foreshore or any of the ships."

"That's right, Watson. And thus the number of possible routes is cut down to a nice little figure. But I must have a few hours' sleep before we take another step, and besides, we cannot do anything until the tide has gone out!"

Holmes, who had been sitting motionless in his comfortable chair, smoking two pipes during the course of his narrative, sprang up from his position, stepped over to his bedroom door and bade me goodnight. I remained seated in front of the fire for a few more minutes, trying to put some order to the things that filled my head. This was a case of lowlifes, semi-criminals and moral decay, and yet Holmes' attitude to the affair was most invigorating. By entering into it, and exploring it in detail, he had managed to put to rest some of my, and perhaps also his, prejudices about the poor people of London. I glanced at the so-called poverty map, still lying outstretched on the breakfast table behind me, and wondered if that survey, conducted by a team of England's foremost scholars, would not have been more accurate if it had been carried out by an unassisted Sherlock Holmes.

I awoke the next morning by a loud knocking on my bedroom door. It was Holmes, ordering me to get up and be in the sitting room in two minutes. I picked up my pocket watch from the bedside table. It was five o'clock.

Holmes was dressed and standing by the breakfast table. It was far too early for breakfast, of course, and Mrs. Hudson was probably still in bed, but on the table, where the breakfast tray usually stood, were two pairs of robust rubber wellingtons.

"There you are, old chap," said Holmes. "Well, into your boots and follow me."

He walked past me out of the door and I could hear him rush down the stairs. I grabbed the boots and, not without some difficulty, pulled them onto my feet. Then I hurried down the stairs and out through the front door. Holmes was already sitting in a hansom cab waiting for us by the curb.

"Chop chop!" he said.

We rode a long way, through a deserted Oxford Street, past Holborn Viaduct and Farringdon, then south through Spitalfields and Whitechapel, before we caught a glimpse of the first of many docks. All through the journey, Holmes remained uncommunicative, merely uttering monosyllabic sounds in reply to my comments.

"It's the boys, don't you think, Holmes? They have turned against young Roger for some reason and bullied him. I know the police constable didn't think them capable of murder, but I'm sure that if the peer pressure is strong enough, that could well be the result. They were waiting for him by the bottom of those steps and then they drowned him."

I looked over at Holmes. He frowned, like someone being interrupted in their sleep.

"I know what you're going to say," I said. "There would have been witnesses to such an assault. But those boys know the docks like the back of their hand! They have hiding places."

Holmes remained silent. He seemed to deliberately ignore me, looking at the passing buildings.

"Holmes!" I said, suddenly realising. "You never looked behind that back door in the opium den! Of course! Mr Fon's son told you what you wanted to hear simply to distract you from investigating that place further."

Now, finally, Holmes turned to me.

"Watson. Do you really think I would have gone out of there without looking behind that door?"

"Oh. So you did? What was behind it, then?"

"Opium."

"I see. And nothing more?"

"Nothing whatsoever."

"Right. Well, at least I managed to get you to talk to me."

The rest of the journey was undertaken in silence.

Three minutes later saw us arriving at the entrance of Pennington Close. Holmes climbed out of the cab before it had come to a full stop and was through the wooden door that led into the side street before I had paid the driver. Coming to this place in the early hours of the morning made me feel that I didn't quite see it as it should be seen. It was virtually deserted apart from a few porters at the far end of it, working odd hours to make ends meet, no doubt. Our first stop was the Shadmore residence, and we found it without any problem, a simple door in a row of many others at the back of a seedy little paved courtyard. Holmes knocked and Walter Shadmore appeared a few minutes later, in the process of putting on his braces.

"Mr 'Olmes," he said. "What on earth is the matter? 'Ave you found my boy?"

"We are about to, Mr Shadmore. If you would accompany us, please."

We waited a moment while Shadmore got properly dressed, and then we continued out of the courtyard and down the street towards the river. When we came to the steps, I observed how the edge of the water had withdrawn quite a bit, leaving the sand bare and allowing us to step down onto the bottom of the river, as it were, and walk among the anchored boats, lying like beached whales around us.

"I've looked down 'ere, Mr 'Olmes," said Shadmore dishearteningly. "There's no way 'e could have come 'ere."

Holmes walked up to him, stuck his hand into his coat pocket and held up something in front of him. It was the Roman coin.

"Mr Shadmore, would you tell me exactly where you found this?"

Shadmore sighed and walked ahead of us a few yards to the west. He looked at the ground in deep concentration before settling on a spot just where the sand bordered on the quay. He kneeled and put his palm on the ground.

"This is the place."

"Just as I thought," said Holmes. "Look."

He pointed with his walking stick at a spot on the wall of the quay, about five foot six inches above the ground. There was a round metal plate there, looking much like a manhole cover, and Holmes started banging on it with his stick. He stopped for a while, and then, to my great astonishment, there was a reply from within.

"Great Scot!" I exclaimed. "Is it the boy?"

Holmes quickly threw off his hat and coat, took an empty wooden crate lying next to him and put it on the ground beneath the metal cover. Standing on it, he managed to get hold of the cover, which was only loosely fastened, and lifted it down, exposing a round hole leading straight into the embankment.

"It must be a sewer," I said.

"Judging from the smell," added Holmes.

As we moved nearer, the first thing we encountered was the smell, but before we could react to it, we noticed a pair of large white eyes staring back at us from the darkness within. Quite soon, the morning light shone on the surrounding facial features, revealing the head of a skinny little boy, looking very frightened and very filthy.

"Dear God!" said Shadmore. "Roger!"

And he climbed up on the wooden crate, reaching into the dark hole and pulled out a small boy in ragged clothes and greasy hair.

"Have you been in 'ere the whole time? Jesus, Roger, I was out 'ere lookin' for ya. Why didn't you call for me?"

The boy looked at his father, then at us, still with the same petrified gaze. Then Holmes pointed with his stick at the boy's left arm, which was bare due to the torn state of his clothes. I recognised the long red wounds as marks from a whipping or a thrashing, and instantly bent down to examine them.

"Who did this to ya, boy?" asked his father.

"Probably the same person he saw in Pennington Close on Tuesday morning, making him run all the way down here to hide."

"Holmes," I said. "These wounds look strange. I don't think they have been caused by a whip or a stick. It's something else, like a piece of clothing."

"A glove?" suggested Holmes.

"Yes, that sounds about right."

Holmes nodded.

"Come, gentlemen. It is time we sought out the mudlark's enemy."

And then he marched away, back to the steps. Mr Shadmore carried his son with him and tried to get him to speak. I tried to comfort them both by assuring them that the wounds would heal, though I was unsure of how deep the mental wounds were, and if they would ever heal. What on earth had frightened this boy so much that he would hide in a stinking sewer for four days? A sewer would be an extremely unpleasant place to be even for a hardened mudlark.

We came to the top of the steps. The docks and the neighbourhood were beginning to awaken, and there were more people in the street than before. Holmes led the way up the street, until he stopped suddenly. In front of him, I could see a stout police constable standing broad-legged in the middle of the street.

"Why, good morning, Constable Morris," said Holmes.

"Good morning, Mr Holmes. Good to see you again."

The exchange of pleasantries was interrupted by the sound of a piercing scream. It was the boy who had caught sight of the policeman. The constable responded to this cry of terror by stepping up to Shadmore with a severe look on his face. Roger tried desperately to creep further into his father's bosom.

"Is this your lad?" he asked Shadmore.

"Yes it is."

Morris shook his head.

"Bad boy, this 'un. Very bad boy."

Holmes put his hand on Morris' shoulder.

"No, Morris. You are the bad one. The way you have tortured this child, both mentally and physically."

"What, me? I've only done me duty! Why, all the constables take the right to reprimand the children in the street if they're misbehavin'. And these boys think they have the run of the street like a gang of hooligans."

"You have overstepped the boundary of decency and the law, Morris. You have systematically beaten him with your police gloves, you have stalked him and directed all your vengeance at one boy."

"He is the worst of the lot! He's a savage, he is!"

"There are many savages in London. Many of them, I'm sad to say, are employed by the police."

"Right, that's it! I shall have you reported. I'm going to the station."

And Morris rushed off, pretending to leave in anger, but in reality trying to escape from justice. Holmes turned to Shadmore and his boy.

"Don't worry about him. We know who he is, and once his superiors hear of his behaviour, he will most certainly be demoted, if not dismissed. You have no reason to fear him anymore, Roger, though I have no doubt your reasons were strong enough, judging from your choice of hiding place, but then again, you were desperate, weren't you? I assume some of the other boys brought you food and drink?"

Roger nodded.

"But why didn't you let them tell me?" asked his father despairingly. "It would have saved me so much worrying, and I could have taught that policeman a thing or two."

180

"When your enemy is the representative of the law," said Holmes, "it is probably quite easy for him to convince a little boy that running off to his parents will not save him. And he probably hid also to save you from trouble, Mr Shadmore."

Shadmore hugged his boy once again and started to walk homewards. Holmes turned to me and smiled.

"It was hardly a complicated case once you allowed yourself to suspect a member of the law enforcement. Our suspicions were initially directed towards Mr Fon or the other mudlarks, but that only reflects our prejudiced view of London. Nothing is ever really black and white, Watson, and there are foes hiding in the police force just as there are friends among the unfortunate."

"I would never have suspected the policeman," I confessed, "but of course you have me at a disadvantage. You had the opportunity to come here and inspect the scene first hand. I only heard about it in the comfort of our sitting room, and a man walking the streets is a much better judge of people than a man sitting in an armchair."

Holmes laughed.

"Precisely, Watson! And sometimes it isn't even enough to walk the streets. You have to disguise yourself as a man of the street as well. Now, Watson, I know a very good pie stand not three blocks from here. We haven't had any breakfast yet and I think we deserve a reward after our good deed. What do you say?"

The Adventure of the Forking Paths

"The nature of mystery," said Sherlock Holmes, "is fraught with ambiguity. For whereas we are generally inclined to seek solutions to our mysteries, man also seems to possess an instinctive urge to allow some puzzles to remain unsolved. And when someone, as occasionally happens, presents a solution to a riddle that everyone formerly agreed was unsolvable, then it is viewed as a breaking of the rules. The answer to a baffling question always contains something of an anti-climax, a disappointment from a humanity that would have preferred to go on searching."

We were seated in our little room at Baker Street, warming our feet by a crackling fire. It was the first really cold day of October, and out on the streets, one was met by the characteristic odour of rotting leaves and damp macadam. Along with the cold came rain, and the last traces of summer's frivolity had been washed away as the people of London started preferring their heated chambers to the sunlit streets. It was barely eleven in the morning and the sparks from the hearth intermingled with the slight patter of rain on our windows. I had been enwrapped in the reading of a Meredith novel, when I was suddenly distracted by Holmes' clear voice.

"So you mean," I said, "that people don't really want solutions to their problems?"

Holmes was sitting curled up in his chair with his dressing gown draped around him like the wrappings of a South American mummy.

"Some mysteries they most definitely want the answers to. They want to know where that valuable emerald brooch that their aunt Nora used to wear has gone. They want to know how to cut down on one's gas bill. On the other hand, I think they prefer to let the big mysteries, those concerning life and death and the universe, remain cloaked in the same shrouds of opacity that have cloaked them since time immemorial. We live in an enlightened age, Watson, where progressions of science succeed one another. It would surprise me very little if we, before this age has drawn to a close, have sought us back to ancient beliefs in fairies or deities or powers of nature."

"That's an unexpected prophecy from a man like yourself."

Holmes smiled.

"On the contrary. In my own mission to solve the problems of everyday life, I may be running errands for the Enlightenment, but if there is one thing I know about solving riddles, it is that the solution often produces a new riddle, and a much more complex one. And so when I consider the velocity with which we answer questions in our time, I feel apprehension for the really large questions that will result from our greedy exploration of the mysteries of the universe."

I was surprised to see my friend in such high spirits. For days he had been occupied with trying to decipher obscure messages in the *Times* agony columns, a business which had left him frustrated and restless, and he had in recent days been less and less inclined to eat or sleep, and more and more inclined to playing feverish nocturnal rhapsodies on his

Stradivarius. But suddenly there was something in his demeanour that led me to think a change in his state of mind was imminent.

"Holmes," I said, putting away my book. "All signs point to the fact that you have a case."

He pierced the air with a lanky index finger.

"Capital, Watson! I see there is no getting around you these days. Well well, I won't test your patience. This arrived by the first post."

He pulled out a folded piece of foolscap from his waistcoat pocket and handed it to me. I opened it and read the message:

"'Dear Mr Holmes, I intend to call upon you today at noon concerning an affair which, as far as I can ascertain, is a mystery without a solution. J L Burgess.' Well, it doesn't reveal much," I said without hiding my disappointment.

"No? Perhaps not, except, of course, that Mr Burgess is left-handed, an experienced botanist and has recently returned from a trip to the Far East."

I gave the paper in my hand a second look. It was small, square and wrinkled.

"All right, Holmes," I sighed. "Let's have it."

Holmes shut his eyes in reaction to my resignation.

"The will to struggle, herr doctor! The energy! Do not give in so easily." He took back the letter. "That the writer is left-handed is evident from a superficial study of the hand-writing, of course. The paper is of a special thin kind made in Japan and not, to my knowledge, sold in Europe. From the scent, I would venture to say that it has been recently purchased. Holding it up to the light reveals the impressions from something written on a paper that has been lying on top of this, and in that text I can discern the Latin names of three rare types of flowers, terms that one doesn't use unless one is a professional. Furthermore, the paper has a weak odour of orchid, probably coming from the hands that have been holding it. That the man has been to Japan, I should think also indicates a certain amount of experience and renown in his field. Now do not chastise yourself, doctor, for failing to observe! The hour is still early, and, in the words of Oscar Wilde: Only dull people are brilliant at breakfast."

It was approaching twelve, and we did not need to wait long before our announced visitor stepped into our chamber. He was a thin and tall man in his early thirties. His long, flaccid hair hung drowsily from a paper-coloured head, framing a visage in which learning had given free reign to concern and nervous tension. He was dressed in a long black frockcoat, and frenziedly shook the raindrops from his umbrella before placing it in our stand. Holmes greeted him heartily.

"Mr Burgess, I presume? Come in, come in."

"I do hope my visit is no interruption to your activities, gentlemen," the young botanist excused himself.

"Not in the least," insisted Holmes. "The disappearance of a plant on the verge of extinction is no trifling matter. Especially not when it concerns one of the finer Japanese orchids, and when the theft has occurred in your own home."

Mr Burgess stepped back.

"So you know what this is about? But my letter revealed nothing. Who has contacted you?"

Holmes raised his hand affably.

"Before I say anything further, I insist that you sit down by the fire. I assure you that your private concerns are safe with me and Dr Watson."

I took the man's hand and felt for myself that he really could do with a bit of warmth. Hence we sat ourselves by the fireplace as Burgess blew his nose in a big white handkerchief.

"If you will allow me to explain," said Holmes, "you will see that my knowledge is not all that sensational. Apart from the inferences I drew from your letter I can see that you have some yellow-coloured spores on your waistcoat lapel. They are pollen from a flower, and since I concluded from your stationary that you have recently visited Japan, it was hardly a bold assumption that you have acquired a plant there. Being a man of passion, you would naturally want to spend as much time as possible with it, and the placement of the spores so high up on your attire suggests to me that they come from a plant that you have recently studied up close. But the spores have not landed there today. Some of them have been smeared into little smudges. You have not touched the plant for at least twenty-four hours and when I add your professional zeal into the equation, I surmise that it must be as a result of circumstances over which you have no power. A robbery."

The botanist looked at his coat sleeve. The little spots were quite apparent at closer study.

"Remarkable. You must possess considerable knowledge in my field."

"Not exactly. I only recognise pollen when I see it. I have, however, written a small pamphlet entitled *Plant*

Pigments and Their Significance in Modern Criminal Investigations."

"Oh yes, I am familiar with it. But tell me, how could you know that the theft has taken place in my own home?"

"Your condition. Hastily tied shoelaces and the way your necktie sits askew on your shirt collar indicates a nervousness of a sort only violations of privacy may awaken. That you had also buttoned every single button in both your overcoat and frockcoat signals to me a man who wishes to shield off the outside world, afraid of what it might do to him. As I'm sure Dr Watson will tell you, our minds sometimes work independently of our consciousness."

I nodded eagerly.

"You make me sound like a very obvious man, Mr Holmes," said Burgess.

"Everything that is visible is obvious."

"You almost save me the trouble of having to tell you about my experiences."

"I beg you to do just that, and leave out no details. My friend and I wish to hear everything!"

Holmes picked up a pipe and leaned back in his chair. Mr Burgess sat at the edge of his seat, looking quite uncomfortable.

"I shall do as you ask. Three days ago I returned home from a lengthy journey of research through China and Japan, taking along a substantial collection of seeds, bulbs and plants home with me. But the treasure of my collection was a specimen of the Apostasia kiro, or Japanese Yellow Shrub Orchid, one of the world's rarest orchids. Its name comes from the curious yellow colour of its petals and it has for centuries been used as a remedy against blindness. I happened upon it in a convent outside Kyoto and I guarded it with my life during the remainder of my journey. Strangely enough, no one showed any interest in it, and I was permitted to transport it without incident back to England, where I immediately started to examine and analyse it.

"I live in a small house in Ashgrove outside of Fenton, together with my wife Sarah and our little boy Eugene, who is five years old. The household consists of a housekeeper, a maid, and a gardener who I have engaged to assist me in the construction of a labyrinth in the back of my garden. You see, my real interest lies in our domestic flora and English gardening traditions, and my trip was done as an assignment for the department where I work, and it is my intention to hand over all my finds to them next week. The temptation to look closer at the beauty of the orchid, however, overpowered me. After my homecoming I took the plant to my study, which is located at the back of the house and has a series of high windows all along the outer wall, overlooking my beloved labyrinth. The windows give me a full view of the winding garden paths, and I very much enjoy sitting at my worktable, raising my eyes now and then to admire the beauty of my creation.

"And so it was here I sat after coming home to work with my orchid. After lunch yesterday, I retreated to my study to work in seclusion. As usual, I locked the door to guarantee my peace and quiet – with a small child in the house you can never be too careful – but since it was a sunny day, and the room, facing south, tends to become quite warm on account of its large windows, I opened one of them to let in the cool autumn air. I was immediately absorbed by my studies, and knowing that I sometimes lose all notion of time when thus immersed, I cannot tell you the exact time when I found it necessary to consult one of the reference works in my adjacent library. I rose from my chair, but can clearly remember that I raised my eyes to glance out across the garden before turning my back to it, and saw no one outside. The labyrinth is quite recently planted and the bushes haven't had time to grow to a full size, which means they are still quite low. Nobody could possible hide among them, but when I returned from the library, after what could only have been thirty seconds, I saw to my great horror that the pot on the desk was gone!

"Mr Holmes, I am a man of weak nerves, and I instantly succumbed to them, but not before looking out through the window, still not seeing a living soul out there. And yet there was no doubting that the orchid had vanished through the open window. The pot was standing only a few inches from it, and nobody could have been hiding in the room. Eventually, I examined the flowerbed below the window but there were no footprints. The window is only a few feet above ground, but the flowerbed is wide, and no one could have reached the window without stepping in the moist soil. After this, I ascertained where the other members of the household had been at the time of the theft. Both the maid and the cook were in the kitchen. The back door leads to the garden, but they were both busy preparing supper at that time, and my suspicions do not fall on them. They are honest, hard-working people who have been in my employ for years.

"Apart from them, there is my gardener. His name is Dunraven. He is an extremely skilled craftsman and he has a passion for botany rivalling my own. But he is a curious sort, and despite his having been with us for a year now, I cannot say I have quite got to know him. He is in his fifties and smells of tobacco. I don't know much about his background."

"And your wife?"

"Bedridden with a slight cold. She is better this morning, but she was in her bedroom all day yesterday and the boy insisted on keeping her company. Oh Mr Holmes, I don't know what to do. The entire mystery seems unsolvable."

"Tell us about the place where you work," asked Holmes.

Burgess shrugged.

"It's a very small institute. We work with the aim of starting a museum and botanical garden and my orchid would have been one of its centre pieces. My closest colleague is Unwin, who specialises in orchids and was very enthusiastic when I told him about my find. He lives here in London, but he is such a good-natured and harmless man that I would not think any ill of him. You must help me. The institute has invested a lot of money in my trip and now all our plans are at risk."

Holmes, who had been sitting as still as a statue during the desperate man's narrative, instantly straightened his back and took his pipe from his mouth.

"You may rest assured, Mr Burgess. Return home and try to get a hold of yourself. Watson and I will arrive this afternoon and then I have every reason to believe we may help you."

Mr Burgess put his palms together.

"Come as quickly as you can. The men from the institute are arriving in a few days to correct the samples, so the sooner the problem is solved the better."

We bid farewell to the troubled botanist, who stepped out into the improving October weather.

"Well, what do you think, Watson? Is Mr Burgess correct? Have we finally encountered a mystery without a solution?"

"It may look like it, but things don't disappear just like that. No, there is something rotten about the whole business. The opened window must be the key."

"That would be the most likely line of reasoning. But I am more fascinated by Mr Burgess' curious maze, and why he would want to construct one. Mazes are never a help in matters of mystery, Watson. No, I don't believe the flower has vanished into thin air either. Not unless Burgess has come into the possession of a truly magical plant."

Following a hasty lunch, we travelled from Paddington towards Fenton on the one thirty-train. Holmes was in a splendid mood, excitedly commenting on the landscape outside the window during the journey. He had recently taken an interest in agricultural history, and was able to point out where features in the terrain indicated previous locations of farmsteads, and virtually invisible lines in the ground that were the remains of old boundaries and enclosures. It was comforting to see him in such a harmonious state of mind.

Upon our arrival in Fenton, we continued by coach to the little village of Ashgrove, where appealing redbrick cottages adorned the roadside with colourful gardens. Burgess' home was one of the larger houses, an imposing dark red lodge watching contemplatively over the surrounding yellow and red foliage like a slumbering giant. As we walked up to the house, a gust of wind caught hold of the branches of a large oak tree, making them sway rhythmically. Holmes put a hand on my arm and looked about.

"This may be a more complicated story than I had thought."

"Really?" I said. "What makes you say that?"

He frowned.

"I don't know. I have very clear hypotheses, and the whole matter seems quite simple, but there is something else. I hate to call it a premonition, but I don't know what other word to apply to it. I think it is best we proceed with caution."

"Caution against what?"

He looked over his shoulder suspiciously, then leaned in and whispered:

"Dead ends."

His lack of confidence unsettled me. During the entire trip, he had appeared tranquil, and I had begun to think that this problem to him was a very simple thing, but now it was as if the atmosphere of this place affected him. It affected me too, but like Holmes, I was unable to put my finger on it. It wasn't impending danger I sensed, only impending disorientation.

Burgess met us in the door. He was calmer than at our last meeting, but despite the improvement of the weather and a rise in temperature, his hand was still cold when I took it. We were shown around the house and introduced to the household. The cook was a hefty old girl whom everyone referred to as Hetty. A dark shade in her eyes told of a woman with a lot of life experience and hard-learned lessons, and she only answered Holmes' questions with low mumblings. The maid was called Emma, and she met us with courtesy and a warm smile. Both of them were troubled by the current situation and probably feared for their jobs more than worrying about a lost flower.

Mrs. Burgess was a charming woman, and when I thought about her union with the frail and silly academic that was her husband, I concluded that Mrs. Burgess had been quite a catch.

"Thank you for taking time to see us, Mr Holmes," she said as she met us in the parlour. "Our home is not at its best in this moment and I hope that you can return it to its usual composure."

But Holmes was not visibly taken in by her gentleness.

"Madam, I have come in the hope of revealing one or two things that are obscure to you, but I can work no miracles. Restoring peace to this home is a task I leave in your hands. Now, if you would show me to the room where the theft took place."

The woman realised that she was addressing a man of fervour, and escorted us through the hallway past the staircase.

"I was in bed resting upstairs, and didn't react until I heard the commotion."

"And the boy?"

"Was in my room until I dosed off, and when I awoke he had run into his room next door, where he was playing with his building bricks when I looked through the door."

Holmes let his gaze sweep across the staircase and hallway just as a small child materialised in a door at the further end of the room. Holmes raised his eyebrows.

"And this is the little rascal, I see. Please to meet you, young sir."

The boy stepped up to Holmes and shyly offered him his hands.

"Eugene," he whispered.

"Good afternoon, Eugene. Sherlock is my name."

Eugene shook his hand slightly, then hid behind his mother's gown and looked suspiciously at us for a while before running out of the room again. Holmes laughed loudly.

"You can't get around children, can you? Don't they show you the meaning of it all?" He rose from his crouched posture. "Let us see that study of yours, Mr Burgess."

We found that Burgess' description of his room had taken the most vital points into consideration. The most striking feature was the row of windows through which the spectacular labyrinth outside could be viewed. To my surprise, Holmes took little interest in the interior of the room and directly stepped up to the worktable where the pot had been standing. He worked his way across the windowsill with his magnifying glass, and muttered with discontent at what he saw.

"Nothing here. Let us have a look in the garden."

"I assure you, Mr Holmes," said Burgess. "There isn't a trace out there."

"Well, at least I shall have the pleasure of strolling in your exquisite garden," replied Holmes. "Remember, we have just come from a grey day in London."

And the garden was actually quite suitable for a leisurely afternoon stroll. From the paved path that cut right through the boxwood hedges, narrower passageways radiated to the left and right in various directions which at first sight appeared chaotic but eventually turned out to be systematic, making up intricate patterns that created a symmetrical and harmonious whole. I had no doubt that it would be very easy to get lost in this maze once it had grown to its full size, but the way it was now, this place certainly did not contain any place for a burglar to hide. Further away from the house were several large bushes and trees through which anyone could have sneaked undetected, but the distance between them and the house was so great that nobody could have run from them to the house and back in the brief time that Burgess turned away from the window. We found our own way to the flowerbed below the study window, and Holmes bent over it. The earth here was moist and soft, and if anyone had stepped here they would most certainly have left an imprint. After having studied petals and stems for damages, Holmes stood up and clapped his hands.

"Stupendous! The thief could not possibly reach the window from the path, but there has been no one walking in this flowerbed in a very long time." He looked upwards. "And there is no access to this window from above, and no upper-floor window directly above it. Ah, but here comes a helping hand!"

Down the middle path came a man looking considerably older than his years, with a worn, tanned face and shabby hair pressed down by a shapeless canvas hat. Around the waist, he wore a dirty apron, and his gait was slow and stumbling.

"Just the man we needed," declared Holmes. "Mr Dunraven, I assume?"

"At your service, sir."

"Has anybody touched this flowerbed since the theft?"

Dunraven shook his head.

"Where were you when the theft occurred?"

"I were yonder i't'shed."

"And what were you doing in the shed?"

"Planting cuttings."

Holmes asked us to show us the shed and the gardener took us there. It was located in a dark corner of the large garden, surrounded by a disarray of broken pots and piles of tools thrown among weeds and compost heaps. This was quite the backstage area of the garden. The shed had no windows and judging by its inside, Dunraven had made it into his home. The walls were covered by illustrations and plans depicting various types of gardens and mazes. Holmes inspected them with a keen eye.

"Tell me, do you have great experience in the laying out of gardens?"

The mysterious man rubbed his chin.

"I once took part in laying out a maze in Cornwall."

"So you know a great deal about mazes, do you?"

"They are the perfect symbol."

"Really? How is that?"

Dunraven stepped out of the shed and started walking back towards the labyrinth that was the framework of our mystery.

"The path leading into the maze divides, again and again, like the possibilities of the universe. In the forked paths hides every eventuality, every alternative. And none. Just as you might find your answers there, you will also find false answers, answers that lead you back to where you started. But above all, there are irrelevant trifles, distractions that take us away from the path, roads that we cannot turn around on, that taunt us and turn us into eternal prisoners in a web of trivialities."

Holmes looked at the philosophical gardener with the gaze of a pathologist who can see his conclusions before he has even begun his autopsy.

"Clever," replied Holmes. "Your outlook on life seems to verge on the radical, but I grant you that we can only follow the train of reason and logic when the trifles add up to make a coherent sum. And when we are unable to follow the train of the reasonable, we might as well follow the train of the unreasonable. Instead of going to the right places, we may systematically go to the wrong places; go down every cul de sac that will only lead us out of the way, because if one has no clue whatsoever, then one might of course just as well rely upon chance, and it is just as likely that that method will lead you to your goal as a systematic and logical method without clues."

I could almost detect the trace of a smile in Dunraven's otherwise stoic face.

"You seem to me a man who has a great deal of luck when he is trapped in a labyrinth."

Holmes chuckled.

"Luck? Ha!"

Dunraven picked up a spade that had been lying on the ground nearby and returned to his shed. Holmes followed him with his eyes, then walked back into the maze. I walked his way.

"We have sought our answers in locked rooms, Watson. But is it not much more difficult to grapple with a place open to every imaginable possibility?"

"Surely you don't agree with all the poppycock that old man was babbling about?" I said.

"I don't think it is a question of agreeing or disagreeing. It is just a question of choosing a view of life and then sticking to it. If you are open to the possibility of everything or, indeed, of nothing, then life is a very unsteady thing. But if you, like me and, I think, you, choose an outlook which is more consistent and based on a set of distinct assumptions, then perhaps you become less tolerant but, on the other hand, mysteries are solved and you can sleep at night. It is merely a matter of how much time you want to spend thinking without reaching any conclusions."

"Well, I'm no philosopher."

"It has nothing to do with philosophy. It's just a matter of finding something to cling on to."

"Cling on to what?"

"The belief in knowledge, rather than oblivion. The proof is in what we see before us. Look here. The bend of the path makes it impossible to look further than a few yards ahead or behind. When these bushes have grown to their full height this will become a truly bewildering labyrinth, but even then it will be able to master. As it is, we only need to keep in mind one simple fact: that no one can pass through it unseen."

"By God, that's true! The thief simply must have gone the way through the labyrinth, even though it is practically impossible to get through unseen. He must have been fully visible during some time."

"Precisely, Watson." Holmes leaned forward, drew his finger across the paved path and then stood up in his full length. "I think we have found something to hold on to."

"What?"

"Reason. A logical chain of circumstances can lead the most perplexed maze-walker on the right path. The riddle, Watson, does not go outside the boundaries of this formidable garden, and the answer can be found here. But now I see our client approaching with his family. Mr Burgess, as you can see, Dr Watson and I are completely entrapped in your labyrinth."

I looked around and noticed that he was absolutely right. On our aimless ramble through the maze while we were discussing the case, we had actually come to a dead end.

"If you would give us directions to come out," continued Holmes, "then I will tell you where you may find your precious orchid."

Slightly amused, Burgess gave us directions that we carefully followed, and we met the little family in the central path.

"Mr Burgess," said Holmes, "I think I can clear up a few things for you."

"Really?" muttered Burgess dejectedly. "I am grateful for all your efforts, but I have a feeling I will not see my Japanese yellow orchid again."

Sherlock Holmes pursed his lips as if to hide a broad smile.

"Am I mistaken if I assume that your birthday is close?"

Burgess opened his mouth.

"Yesterday was my thirty-fifth birthday! How could you know that?"

"If you would be so good as to lower your gaze and examine the flowerbed on your left. There you will find a somewhat delayed birthday present."

Burgess frowned and bent his head, tired of jokes. Within seconds, his face went through a transformation and his legs folded to the point where he fell down on his knees in the middle of the garden path.

"My orchid! My dear orchid!" He pointed violently at an unassuming little flower planted in the wet soil right beside the pavestones. "There it is. Has it been there the whole time? But how has it ended up here? Unless it jumped down from the window and walked down the path, I cannot grasp it!"

Holmes looked seriously at Mrs. Burgess.

"I believe, my dear, that the key to the mystery is right behind your back."

Astonished, the woman stepped aside, and our looks fell on little Eugene, Burgess' five-year old boy, who blushed and looked down on the ground.

"Don't be shy, boy," Holmes demanded, sounding like an old headmaster trying to be gentle. "Come forward."

Eugene walked up to his father, who in his current posture, was about the same height.

"I just wanted to do something nice for father on his birthday."

Burgess looked puzzled.

"You have been the victim of nothing more threatening than your son's concern," explained Holmes. "What could be a better present for a man like yourself than a helping hand in the garden? Unfortunately Eugene didn't realise the orchid was not meant for this garden."

"But Eugene," said Burgess, embracing the child. "Why didn't you say anything?"

"You became so sad. And then there was a turmoil, and these men came. I was scared."

"And if it had not been for the hedgerows of your labyrinth," said Holmes, "which would not hide the approach of a full-grown thief, but were more than enough cover for your son, you would probably have seen your son on his knees, digging in the garden."

Burgess came to his feet.

"How on earth did this solution come to you, Mr Holmes?"

"What at first seemed like an unsolvable mystery turned out to be one of the simplest I have ever encountered. There were no footprints in the flowerbed below your window, which made the whole thing inexplicable. But upon closer inspection, I found four circular holes in the soil placed in a square about fifteen inches apart. Undoubtedly the imprints made by the legs of a chair. And who would need a chair to be able to reach up to a ground-floor window? Evidently the same person who remained invisible among these low bushes. Excluding all other possibilities, such as Dunraven and your wife, I took a walk here in your maze and came upon your orchid. It wasn't strange to think that your son had acted out of kindness and that the cause was some special occasion. Knowing how children often think a great deal of birthdays that was my guess."

"Marvellous," laughed Burgess. "I am so grateful for your insights, Mr Holmes."

"I don't think you should thank me."

"You're quite right." He lifted his son and let him sit on his arm. "Thank you for thinking of me on my birthday, Eugene. I'm sorry if I frightened you."

Mrs. Burgess stepped up and took her husband's vacant arm.

"Maybe this will teach you to give as much attention to your family as to your work."

Holmes raised his finger.

"And that mysteries always have solutions," he added.

Holmes and I left the Burgess family in peace to allow them to restore their idyll. But as we were travelling back to London, I couldn't help but wonder why Holmes had lost himself in Mr Burgess' labyrinth.

Holmes yawned and closed his eyes.

"Sometimes, my friend, it is necessary to lose one's way in order to find it."

It could hardly have been more than two o'clock in the morning when I was awoken from my sleep by a dreadful noise on the ground floor. Irritated, I crawled out of my bed, put on a robe and stepped out of my room. On the landing below, I could see the silhouette of Sherlock Holmes by the light emanating from our sitting room, and opposite him two men, one of whom was in a dreadful state. Propped up on the shoulder of his companion, he moaned audibly while wiping what looked like blood from wounds on his face.

Holmes looked up towards me.

"Watson," he said. "I think you had better come down."

Without a word, I fetched my medical bag and joined the others in our little consulting room. Mrs. Hudson was in the doorway, looking more angry than anxious about the commotion, and Holmes calmed her down, persuading her to go back to bed and not worry. We went up to the small circle of furniture by the fireplace, where the suffering man was helped down on the chaise-longue by the other visitor, who I now identified as Inspector Bradstreet of Scotland Yard. He turned towards Holmes and me with a concerned look. He was a reasonable and professional man, but the situation had left him breathless, and he searched for words before speaking.

"Mr Holmes, this affair is of such a curious nature that I took the liberty of calling upon you at once without going to the station first. A man on the beat found this gentleman unconscious in the street and as he came to, he insisted on talking to you in person. I suppose Dr Watson might be of help in this matter too."

The man on the chaise-longue squinted at the three men who leaned over him with pathological interest.

"Are you Signor Holmes?" he asked with his eyes fixed on my friend. The accent was decidedly southern, quite probably Italian.

"I am," said Holmes. "Signor…?"

"Perinelli. Alfredo Perinelli. Rare book dealer from Rimini."

Holmes nodded.

"That you are a book-learning man I can see from your fingertips." He caught hold of the man's hands and held them to the light from a paraffin lamp I had just lit. "The many little cuts from a short-bladed paper knife, from all those occasions on which you have cut the pages of a book."

The Italian smiled.

"How astute. And judging from your own fingers, I can see that you are a smoker. Don't let me stop you from lighting a cigarette while you listen to my story."

Holmes had produced a cigarette from the pocket of his dressing gown before the man had finished his sentence.

"First I must insist that my good friend the doctor has a look at those bruises of yours."

I stepped up and opened my medical bag on the sideboard. The man had been brutally beaten in the face by a man's fist. The blemishes were distinct and in some places the swelling had given way to open wounds. But the more I examined this man's face, the more peculiar did his injuries seem to me. As the marks from the blows were quite apparent, I could tell with some certainty where about the face the strikes had landed. In some places you could even tell that it was a left hand that had delivered the blows. But the strange thing was, that the imprints from this left hand were only on the left side of the face, which would mean that the culprit must have been very oddly placed in relation to Signor Perinelli.

I shared my conclusions with the others. Bradstreet appeared surprised.

"We found him in an extremely narrow passageway with very little space for a great struggle. And deeming by the way Mr Perinelli, was lying the other person must have been standing directly in front of him and very close."

I started.

"No no no. He must have been standing just to one side of Signor Perinelli. Or possibly slightly behind him."

"Impossible," the inspector mumbled. "Completely impossible."

We were both taken aback.

"Signor," said Holmes. "What can you recall from the attack?"

"Nothing," admitted the victim. "Absolutely nothing."

Holmes frowned.

"Very well. Tell us about the circumstances."

Perinelli pulled himself up into a seated position and thought for a minute.

"Two weeks ago I had a letter from a colleague of mine here in London. He is an old friend and he is well aware that I specialise in old editions of Italian poets, especially the Provençal poets, who have been my passion ever since I first read La Divina Commedia as a young man to console myself after an unhappy love entanglement. Imagine my surprise, gentlemen, when my colleague Ponsonby wrote to me to tell me that he had come across a handwritten manuscript containing the first three cantos of Inferno! It is a well-known fact that there is not one single handwritten page by the great Dante Alighieri left behind, and the eventuality that something like that would turn up is of course utterly fantastic. Ponsonby wrote that he was not fully qualified to say if the manuscript was by Dante himself, but that it was without question from his time, and that I really ought to take my time to come to London and examine it.

"As I am sure you understand, I did not hesitate to pack my bags and go to London by the first available train. Ponsonby had also implied in his letter that it was possible for me to purchase this manuscript if I should so wish, and this possibility made me as giddy as a schoolboy. Ponsonby received me yesterday when I arrived in your town, and we went immediately to his shop, where I was shown the five-hundred year old papers. Ponsonby claimed to have bought them from an old Spanish rag dealer who had no notion of what it was he had in his possession. When I saw the manuscript, I could not believe my eyes. It was most certainly genuine! And furthermore, the cantos written down on it were earlier versions that no one has ever before seen. I consequently had no doubt that these were papers from the great poet's own writing desk. Perhaps I should have asked myself why it was that they had suddenly reappeared after so many years, but my enthusiasm prevented me, and I bought it without hesitation from my good colleague. Ponsonby was very happy for me, and insisted that we go out and celebrate the deal.

This we did and the hour grew late. I had placed the documents carefully in the inside pocket of my coat, wrapped inside a protective leather folder, so as not to damage them, and there they were during the entire evening, until I rose from the table to return to my hotel. Ponsonby bade me farewell, and we made plans to meet the next day.

The way to my hotel turned out to be much longer than I had anticipated, and my lack of knowledge of the London streets caused me to lose my way among the many alleyways and back streets. This is the last thing I can remember. I must have been attacked shortly after that and robbed of my valuable manuscript. But the only man who knew that I had it was Ponsonby, and I refuse to believe that he would do this to me only for the money."

Holmes had been standing by the window during Perinelli's account. I was sitting next to the poor Italian and mulled over what he had said. There were very few clues in this mystery, but one thing did strike me.

"What do you think of the rag dealer who sold the documents to your colleague?" I asked. "Could he have had his eye upon you the whole time? Maybe he found out what had slipped through his hands and wanted it back?"

Perinelli shook his head.

"Ponsonby claimed that he had only taken his money so that he could board a ship soon after and return to his native country. He was something of a tramp, and also old and weak. I could not suspect him of it."

Bradstreet cleared his throat.

"In that case I only see one option. Mr Perinelli is the victim of a random attack and the perpetrator simply emptied his pockets after beating him unconscious."

Perinelli smiled joylessly.

"He seemed to have missed my pocketbook and gone straight to a bundle of papers that could have been quite without value."

"Are you certain about Signor Perinelli's injuries, Watson?" asked Holmes.

I was somewhat surprised to hear that he was still thinking about that detail.

"Quite certain," I said. "I'm no expert in the field, but in this case it seems rather straightforward. The man who struck Perinelli must have been standing next to him."

"It cannot be," insisted Bradstreet.

"In that case I can see no other solution," I said, "than that the man had only a left arm and incredible strength in it. In that way he may have been able to hit Perinelli with his left hand from straight ahead."

Holmes laughed.

"A one-armed boxer? That should be quite easy to find. And one that has a special interest in medieval manuscripts. No no, we need to look at the problem from a different angle." He turned back towards the window and stood there for a while, in silence, before glancing at our visitor as a police-court judge might peer at a petty criminal. "Signor, would you call yourself a healthy individual?"

Perinelli looked at us all with a puzzled expression.

"Yes. Just as healthy as the next man, I suppose."

"Come, come. Tell us," Holmes persisted.

"Tell you what?"

Holmes looked at him.

"About your accident."

"How could you…" Perinelli sighed. "Yes. It is true that I have had an accident recently. But I can't see…"

Holmes glanced at me, and now I was actually beginning to see what he was after.

"Did you hit your head?" I said.

"Yes," replied Perinelli. "It happened a few days ago in my shop in Rimini. In a corner there was an old bookshelf that had been standing there since I inherited the shop from my father. I reached up for a book and the entire shelf collapsed. Several heavy volumes toppled down on me, literally burying me on the floor. When I came to, my head hurt, but I was relatively unharmed. No reason to call for a doctor. But what does this have to do with the robbery?"

"It has everything to do with the robbery," said Holmes. "Because it was then that it began."

"What are you on about, man?" cried Bradstreet. "This is pure conjecture."

"On the contrary," said Holmes. "It is fact. In reality, you don't remember a single thing from your stay in London do you, Signor Perinelli?"

Perinelli held his gaze locked in the distance.

"But it must have been like that! This is no dream. I am here, in London."

Holmes looked at me.

"Shall I explain or will you? After all, it is a doctor's expertise."

I insisted that Holmes should explain, since I hadn't yet put all the pieces together in my head.

"The accident to your head was more serious than you thought, Signor, because it caused a particularly bad case of falling sickness."

"Falling sickness?"

"Epilepsy, as it is sometimes referred to," I remarked. "The symptoms in your case are quite plain. A seizure is preceded by several days of weariness and nausea, and afterwards you generally don't remember a thing of what has happened in the past few days."

"Falling sickness is often caused by serious head injuries," continued Holmes, "and since you are apparently unaware that you are suffering from it, I concluded that you have contracted the condition quite recently, probably as a result of an accident. The final attack was for you particularly violent, maybe enhanced by the alcohol you had consumed just before, and your extremities were shaking so much, that you managed to hit yourself unconscious by striking yourself several times with your left hand. That is the only reasonable explanation to the mystery of the one-armed pugilist."

"But what about the manuscript? And Dante?"

"Following a seizure, your thoughts and perceptions may end up in complete disarray, and hallucinations are mistaken for truths," I commented.

"But why should I go all the way to London?"

Holmes scratched his forehead.

"You can really only answer that yourself."

It was quite an awkward moment. Bradstreet helped the confused man to sit up straight on the chaise-longue. He touched the wounds on his face carefully and seemed to ponder for a bit. Then, as if entertaining some private thoughts that amused him, he grinned.

"You remind me a bit of Dante yourself, Signor Holmes. When Boccaccio met Dante at Ravenna he was so struck by his appearance that he would write a description of him a few years later: 'He was of average height, and, advanced in his years, was somewhat stooped, solemn and gentle in movement, and always dressed in simple garb suited to his mature years. His face was long, his nose aquiline, and his eyes large rather than small; he had a great jaw, and his lower lip protruded beyond the upper; his expression always melancholic and pensive.' It could be a description of you, Signor Holmes. I have often thought of the parallel when I have read about your exploits."

Holmes smiled, looking out of the window.

"I think I am starting to remember why I came to London," continued Perinelli. "It seems that your revelation has opened the gates to my memory. When I was but nine years old, I fell in love with a woman for the first time. I loved her from a distance with a strength like that of Dante and Petrarch, but she could never be mine, and soon her family moved from our town. One week ago, I received a letter from her. She wrote that she was now living in London, that I had always been on her mind, and that now, when her husband had passed away, she could see me again, if I still wanted to see her. It was with this letter in my pocket and the warm feelings it left in my heart that I came to London, gentlemen. I was propelled by my undying love. But I was much too nervous to see her immediately, so I went to visit my old friend Ponsonby and together we went to a public house. There was never any manuscript. Perhaps my reawakened love made me associate everything a bit too much with Dante. Or maybe I unconsciously wanted to see the man who is his image while I was in London."

The Italian's story was touching for both Bradstreet and me. He told it with such sadness and emotion that I felt a tear in the corner of my eye. Holmes was standing with his back turned against us, looking out of the window.

"I was so consumed by love," said Perinelli, "that I could not think about whether I had sustained any injuries from the collapsing bookcase. I will never retrieve a manuscript by Dante – ha! the thought of it – but I still haven't visited her, and maybe I can find what Dante wrote about but never found himself. He was doomed to live apart from the woman he loved, and he was compelled to walk through the seven circles of hell to reach her. Sometimes your city feels like an inferno, if you don't mind my parallel. In some quarters you think you have come to the very lowest circle. Imagine that Dante's fantasies would one day come so close to realisation." He laughed. "London is a lonely place. The people here are alone. They wander through inferno, but they never reach purgatory. 'Nel mezzo del cammin di nostra vita mi ritrovai per una selva oscura.'"

Holmes turned away from the window.

"'Considerate la vostra semenza: fatti non foste a viver come bruti, ma per seguir virtute e canoscenza'," he replied.

Perinelli smiled once more, a very different man from when he had arrived. Bradstreet and I helped him up from the chaise-longue.

"I thank you, gentlemen, for your help."

"Best of luck," I said and took him by the hand.

He nodded with a certain amount of concern in his eyes, but also a dash of hope, and then he was escorted from the room by the police inspector. This story had delighted me, and I was once again at peace after that brutal awakening. I turned to Holmes with a sigh.

"I'm going back to bed, Holmes."

Holmes crept up in his armchair and lit a new cigarette. He kept his eyes focused on the paraffin lamp in front of him.

"Do that, Watson."

I knew he would remain there, well past dawn, and he wouldn't be sleeping. I knew it, even though I couldn't understand it. I was very tired myself.

Also from MX Publishing

MX Publishing is the world's largest specialist Sherlock Holmes publisher, with over a hundred titles and fifty authors creating the latest in Sherlock Holmes fiction and non-fiction. From traditional short stories and novels to travel guides and quiz books, MX Publishing cater for all Holmes fans. The collection includes leading titles such as *Benedict Cumberbatch In Transition* and *The Norwood Author* the winner of the 2011 Howlett Award (Sherlock Holmes Book of the Year). MX Publishing also has one of the largest communities of Holmes fans on Facebook with regular contributions from dozens of authors.

www.mxpublishing.com

Also from MX Publishing

 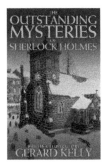

Our bestselling short story collections 'Lost Stories of Sherlock Holmes' , 'The Outstanding Mysteries of Sherlock Holmes', 'Untold Adventures of Sherlock Holmes' (and the sequel 'Studies in Legacy) and 'Sherlock Holmes in Pursuit'.

Also from MX Publishing

A Study in Regret

What if two had perished at Reichenbach Falls? One simple, disastrous error throws Sherlock Holmes from his intended Hiatus into a tortuous journey of sorrow and remorse. Far from home, broken in body and spirit, the haunted detective fights to survive the single most tragic failure of his career - a fight he cannot win alone.

www.mxpublishing.com

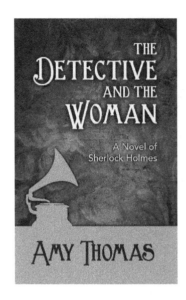 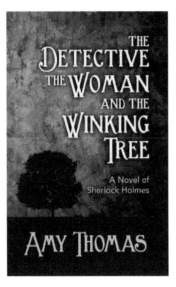

Links

MX Publishing are proud to support the Save Undershaw campaign – the campaign to save and restore Sir Arthur Conan Doyle's former home. Undershaw is where he brought Sherlock Holmes back to life, and should be preserved for future generations of Holmes fans.

Save Undershaw   www.saveundershaw.com

Sherlockology   www.sherlockology.com

MX Publishing   www.mxpublishing.com

You can read more about Sir Arthur Conan Doyle and Undershaw in Alistair Duncan's book (share of royalties to the Undershaw Preservation Trust) – *An Entirely New Country* and in the amazing compilation Sherlock's Home – The Empty House (all royalties to the Trust).

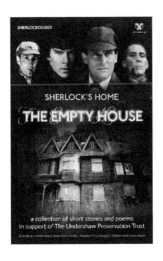